To Lill,
Trust God! He loves
you.

Alisha Karpal

THE TALES OF FIFTEEN

ALISHA KARPOL

Order this book online at www.trafford.com
or email orders@trafford.com

Most Trafford titles are also available at major online book retailers.

Printed in the United States of America.

ISBN: 978-1-4269-6589-0 (sc)
ISBN: 978-1-4269-6590-6 (hc)
ISBN: 978-1-4269-6591-3 (e)

Library of Congress Control Number: 2011909193

Trafford rev. 09/01/2011

 www.trafford.com

North America & international
toll-free: 1 888 232 4444 (USA & Canada)
phone: 250 383 6864 ♦ fax: 812 355 4082

This book is dedicated with gratitude to our Lord Jesus Christ for the gift of writing. My sincere thanks go to Joey, Adam and Jonathan, my dear Grandsons, who so generously gave of their time for help with my computer.

BORDER CROSSING NO. 1

Way back when my parents owned a place down in Phoenix, I would take my two children there during spring break on a holiday. Since my Dad assured me that he'd run the car wash while I was away, I felt it would be okay to leave.

Unfortunately, because money was at a premium at that time and we didn't have enough to pay for several hotels along the route, I ended up driving all the way through from Phoenix to Edmonton which is about a 35 to 40 hour drive.

Occasionally the only peace I could get was when the kids were asleep and I could pull over and catch a few winks myself. On this one trip, by the time I got to the border crossing in Alberta it took about 32 hours of steady driving. I was, needless to say, very tired. And because the children were with me and the trunk of the car was packed with stuff, the car was sitting at a 90 degree angle as I slid to a stop at the border crossing in Sweetgrass, Montana. There was only one mean old guy on duty at the crossing.

"What have you got in the trunk?" he asked me.

"Well, you know with kids, you have to take lots of toys and lots of clothes, because we were gone for two weeks."

He glared at me. "Have you anything to declare?"

So I thought ... better to declare something than to lie and say I have nothing. I call it the comfort zone because you can always say, "Gee, I forgot about that item, and, uh-h-h, that's another one ... and I forgot about that one too," in case someone happens to check. At least I'm semi-truthful about the whole thing because with an answer like that the border agents will simply surmise that you really can't help it if you're stupid. That's the way I've always looked at it.

So this particular time, I decided that I would declare $325.00 bucks worth of goods. It was just a number that came to me. I never kept any of the receipts, because I was afraid that if I knew that the actual total was more than $325.00 bucks, I'd be nervous. The only hope I had was to mark the price of the clothes, which had the original price tags still on them, to a ridiculously low amount, so as to keep my purchases under $325.00.

I noticed the place looked fairly busy. There were a couple of people in front of me, and they'd been pulled over. At the moment, the customs officer had his hands full and looked quite exasperated. He turned to me.

"You'll have to go in, fill out a proper declaration and pay your dues if you're over the limit."

So I thought okay, I'll do the decent thing and fill out the declaration. So I went inside, and same as the outside, there was only one officer on duty.

I noticed that the first two people in the line were a couple of young boys. The Customs officer looked at them warily, "Do you have anything to declare?"

One of the young men replied, "Well, not really."

"And what does "not really" mean? How long have you been gone?"

"Just a few hours."

"What did you buy? Did you buy a tank of gas?"

"Yes, we bought a tank of gas," he said, sarcastically.

"Did you buy anything else?"

"Yeah, I bought a case of beer."

The Customs Officer looked up. "Well, that's gonna cost ya."

"Well, what da'ya mean by that?"

"Well, you have to be in the States overnight."

"Well, maybe I was."

"Then show me a hotel receipt, or a gas receipt that's dated from the day before."

Of course he couldn't produce any receipts because he'd just told the officer that he'd only been there a few hours. He'd bought the beer because it was cheaper by about half price than in Canada. The young man looked at the Customs Officer, speechless.

"Well, you know, I'm going to have to charge you tax on that beer." The customs officer shook his head and calculated the tax which came to $12.50 for the beer.

The young man's mouth dropped. "But that's more than a case of beer would cost in Canada!"

"That's exactly my point, why drive for hours and pay for gas when you can buy it cheaper here!"

Listening to their interaction, I began to shake a little. Directly in front of me was an older man, a lady and their son. They came up to the counter and the agent asked them, "Do you have anything to declare?"

The older man spoke up and said, "Well, you know, just the usual proverbial thing that your wife buys ... uh-h-h, nothing very much."

"Sir, I notice that you have American license plates on that vehicle you have parked out there."

"Well, yeah."

"Is that vehicle yours?"

"Yeah, I bought it."

"Well, where did you buy it?"

"On my trip," he answers, indignantly.

"How did you get a license plate?"

"I have a buddy that owns a house down in Utah and the guy let me use his address, so I thought, since I had to get this car home the only thing I could do was to borrow my friend's license plate on a 24 hour transit, so I could register it in Canada. I'm not lying to you, that's exactly what happened."

The agent looked surprised. "How much was the car?"

The old man looked offended. "None of your damn business how much I paid for the car!"

The agent stopped short. "You have to declare this car, you can't just bring in a car without declaring it."

"You know what? I don't have to tell you nothing. I bought the car with cash money. I got a good deal on it! And now you're trying to make a big deal of it! It's not gonna happen."

The agent stood his ground. "Well, sir, if you don't declare the car, the car will be seized, and you can probably buy it back at the public auction. Or you can declare the car and pay the duty on it. If not, you'll have to leave it here."

The old man stared at him. "This is total bananas. I never heard such crap. You mean to tell me that I can't buy a car in the States and bring it back? A car that I paid for with my own cash money?"

"Yeah, that's exactly right. That's exactly how the law works."

"Well, that's a bunch of horse dung."

"Sir, do you have the bill of sale?"

"Oh, I got the bill of sale. I need that because I have to insure the vehicle back home."

"Well, what did you pay for it?"

"Like I told you before, none of your damn business! ... Okay, okay, I paid a thousand dollars for the car."

"Sir, what year and what make is the car?"

"It's a 2000 Chrysler Intrepid."

"You paid a thousand dollars for a 2000 Chrysler Intrepid?"

"Oh yeah, I did."

"I'm sorry, this is how this works, show me a receipt for a $1,000.00 for the car. A legitimate receipt! Or we do fair market value on the car... in Canadian dollars. And that's what you're gonna pay to get it back!"

The old man looked at the agent stunned.

In the mean time, I stood listening to their dialogue which took about forty five minutes.

The old man finally pulled the receipt out of his pocket. It showed that he'd paid $8,000.00 for the car.

The Customs Officer worked out the duty which came to $1,250.00. A ridiculous amount because the old man had to pay G.S.T. as well as duty on it.

By now the old man was quite angry. "Well, what the hell d'ya think, I carry twelve hundred and fifty dollars in my back pocket? I just finished telling you I put all my money on that car. You think they're gonna take a cheque from me from Canada?"

At this point the customs officer pointed to a spot outside. "I don't care what you paid for the car. Park the car over there. And you're not getting the car back until you pay the bill."

"Well, this is horse crap!" He said as he walked away with his wife and son to discuss how to pay the bill.

The Customs Officer turned to me. "Next."

By then, remembering the paltry goods I'd bought over and above the exemption, I didn't feel half bad after what I'd just witnessed. I declared every item I bought and ended up paying $12.00 in duty.

As I was about to leave, I noticed that the man had returned with the money that he and his wife and son had scraped up. They'd counted out every last dollar they had on them, as well as all their change. It just doesn't pay to get smart with a Customs Officer.

THE END

BORDER CROSSING ...NO. TWO

I had just recently purchased a P.T. Cruiser, and if you're not aware of the size of that car, it's not overly big. And if you take out the back seat, it's more like a higher station wagon. I run a car wash with my Dad. I'd heard of a Car Wash convention in Las Vegas and Elaine and I decided to go. Usually my Dad goes, but this time he couldn't make it, so I went with Elaine.

Elaine, my sister-in-law, didn't think that it was safe for a woman to be traveling alone, so she came with me and said she'd help me with the driving.

Three things we kept in mind ... we didn't have a lot of time, number two ... we didn't have a lot of trunk space, and number three ... we were trying to do it on the cheap.

So we decided that we'd sleep in the back of the Cruiser on the way down, as well as when we got there.

"Why pay for a hotel ?" I said to Elaine, "when we have a perfectly adequate spot in the back of this car."

Neither she nor I considered the fact that we did have luggage and it would be more than lumpy to sleep on. But Elaine said that she had a foam mattress and we'd lay it on the bottom of the P.T. and pile everything else on top, and keep a stretch open where one of us could lay out if we were tired.

That seemed all right because we both take our pillows with us when we travel. The problem was that she couldn't find that foam mattress, so she brought 12 blankets instead. Now I can tell you that blankets, even 12, compared to a foam mattress do not work the same way.

But we started out and it seemed fine. We got as far as the state of Nevada and I made it all the way to Henderson before Elaine took over driving the P.T. I'd driven for a very long stretch, so I was relieved when she offered to drive while I slept for a while. Elaine had never driven my car before. What happened was that she wasn't used to the car and after she turned on the cruise control, she didn't know how to turn it off. She had it set to cruise between 65 and 70 miles an hour.

In front of us there was a big semi-trailer and the road was very hilly. So the P.T. would climb uphill at 70 miles per hour and it would go downhill at 70 miles per hour. Now the semi did the opposite. It went full speed downhill and lost speed going uphill. So Elaine kept moving to the fast lane going uphill and back to the slow lane going downhill with the semi passing her each time she went downhill. So she just kept going back and forth, back and forth, while I was trying to sleep. After about 45 minutes of being tossed around, I decided it was time to take over.

"Elaine, I'm feeling pretty good now and I think I can drive another five hours."

She happily let me drive because she was tired of the semi passing her all the time.

When we got to Vegas we attended one Car Wash meeting, then began to think about some serious shopping. The whole idea was that we were supposed to get some new input at the convention ... something related to the car wash. But we got sidetracked and went shopping instead.

Elaine decided that she had to buy one of those Panasonic vibrator chairs ... the really big ones. She found one that even had it's own foot stool attached. It came all in one piece. By a turn of a switch it not only vibrated, but went up and down as well. What a find! The chair was on sale for $1,200.00 U.S.

So she phoned Ted, her husband, to tell him about it, but she was too nervous to tell him the price. "Ted, I was wondering if you'd mind if I bought a chair?"

There was a moment's hesitation. "Elaine, why are you buying a chair in Las Vegas? How are you going to get it back? Or are you having it shipped back?"

"No, but Carol and I figured that there'd be enough room at the back of the P.T. "

"Oh, then it can't be that big. How expensive is it?"

Elaine paused. "It's on special." But she wouldn't say how much.

"Is it a good deal? Do you really need it?"

Elaine never did tell Ted how much the chair really was, but he assumed it would be a reasonable price ... maybe $300.00.

We tried to keep track of our receipts and how much we were spending, so we'd know how much to declare at the border. At that point we'd spent from about $1,500.00 to $2,000.00 U.S. each. Even so, Elaine made up her mind to buy the chair.

We figured that with the big hatch open in the back, we might get that monster chair inside the car, somehow.

We decided to leave early the next morning. But first we'd have breakfast ... and right after breakfast we'd pick up the chair because we couldn't leave it unattended in the car all night because someone might steal it. Then right after picking it up, we'd leave for home. That was the plan.

We got to the store right after doing some more shopping and of course we were a little late to get a really early start, because by now it was almost 10:00 A.M.

As soon as we walked in the clerk told us, "Oh, I'm sorry, but Doug, he's the one who sold you the chair, just went for his break. He should be back in about 20 minutes."

So, since he wasn't there, we went shopping again. Pretty soon an hour and a half had gone by and well past the 20 minutes. So we went back to the store and asked the clerk about Doug again, and she said, "I'm sorry, but he's out to lunch."

"Out to lunch?"

I mean we still had to drive home, this time straight home because there was no room for even one person to lay in the back because we had all the other stuff we'd bought packed in there and it already more than filled the back even without the chair. So I figured that if we could pile things on top of the chair, on the side of the chair, under the chair, you know, somehow we'd make room.

It was already three in the afternoon and getting late ... so we figured we might as well go for lunch some place where we could find a buffet, so we could eat quick. As soon as we finished lunch, we went back to the store because we really had to get going.

The clerk was there but not Doug. "I'm sorry, you just missed him, he's on his break now. But he should be back in about five minutes."

So rather than shopping, this time we decided that maybe we should wait. We waited for about five minutes before he came back. He brought out a very big box with the chair already packed inside. It was a huge box. We'd only seen the floor model and it didn't look all that big.

At this point, I mentioned to him that we'd need an extra receipt and if he could leave it blank we would appreciate it. "We can't really say at Customs that we've paid $1,200.00 for this chair because we'd have to pay a lot of duty on it," I explained to him. So, since he wanted to make the sale, he gave us a couple of blank receipts.

Then he got out the dolly and wheeled the chair in the box out to the parking lot. He took one look at the P.T. and said, "Ladies, you're crazy if you think that chair will fit in there. Look at all the stuff you've already got!"

So we took everything out and I said to him, "I think there's enough room now. But you'll have to take it out of the package, obviously." So we pushed and pulled and angled the chair inside. Even without the box, with great difficulty, it cleared by about a quarter of an inch. Then we piled everything back in. We filled the back right up to the ceiling. We couldn't even recline the seats and the P.T. was now sitting tilted at a peculiar angle.

By now it was 6:30 at night and Ted phoned again. "So where are you girls? Are you as far as Salt Lake City?"

Elaine explained, "No, not exactly. Actually, well, right now I'm just looking out the window and I can still see the lights of Vegas."

I can't imagine what Ted must have thought.

We carried on driving. Though I'd been shopping for eight hours, this time I couldn't lay down even if I'd wanted to because there just wasn't any room.

After a time, I said to Elaine, "So what are you going to declare at the border?"

Since Elaine is a pack rat, she had saved every receipt known to man and had them laid out on a tray in front of her. The receipts were sorted into different piles and for the last half hour she kept busy sorting them and resorting them.

She looked worried. "I don't know what to do. We're only allowed $250.00 Canadian, so what do you think it actually looks like?"

I looked behind me. Everything was packed in so tight I couldn't see the back window. "Well, I think a little more than two-fifty."

Elaine became so upset, she was ready to cry.

So I said, "Why don't you add up all you've got without the chair. After that we'll see."

She shook her head. "You know, I'm really tired right now. I think I'll take a nap."

It was her way of handling things. This already happened three times on the trip. The third time she told me that she was going to nap we were coming very close to the border, so I said to her, "Do something quick because you're running out of time."

She looked down at her tray and began sorting through the receipts again, carefully examining each one. After some time, she added up $600.00 without the chair.

For myself I calculated $1,500.00. So it looked like we'd both be well over on the exemption. We decided right then and there that rather than go through the Coutts, Montana, crossing, we'd try a different way, a much less traveled route that doesn't get too much traffic. It wasn't even on the map, but we'd both heard of it. So we made a turn in the road and after driving over miles and miles of hills, it took us an extra three hours to find it.

Again Elaine lined up her receipts.

"You might as well throw some of those out. They won't do you any good," I told her.

She nodded. "You know, I just have to close my eyes again, I've got a headache." With that her head dropped to her chin and her eyes shut while she took another quick nap. I didn't want her to have a headache, so I let her sleep.

"Elaine, wake up, we're getting pretty close," I said, getting anxious.

She merely nodded, her eyes still closed. "Hm'm'm."

"Elaine we're getting really close now. You're going to have to decide how much to claim."

"Hm'm'm." Suddenly she came awake. "Pull over!"

"Elaine, if you couldn't decide on anything in twenty-four hours, I don't think another ten minutes more is going to make any difference. So how much do you think you've got?"

"I don't know."

"Just add it quickly. Roughly. Do the simple math. You must have some idea by now."

Of course since I'd never taken that route before ... all of a sudden we turned a corner and voila! There it was directly in front of us! The border crossing! And standing outside with her hands on her hips was a female Customs Agent.

It looked almost like she was waiting for us.

Elaine yelled, "Pull over!"

"I can't! If I pull over now they're going to be more than a little suspicious. Rather than pull over, I think I'll drive really slow and you're going to have to decide on a figure real fast."

"So what shall I put down for the chair?"

"Elaine, write something down! I don't care what you write! And you can't have the receipt on you. And don't throw it out the window, it'll look too obvious."

Elaine took the receipt, rolled it up and put it down the vent of the car. We never did find it even after we got home. Then she took out the blank receipt that Doug, our obliging salesman, had given us and looked at me. "Well, what shall I write?"

"Uh-h-h, how about "Mother's Day Special." I think about ... write about $500.00."

"$500.00? Are you sure? Did you forget? It cost $1200.00." She was shaking like a leaf.

"You know, that'll work as long as that lady out there doesn't pull that chair out. Now calm down! ... Calm down!"

So I pulled up and tried to look casual. As luck would have it there were only two women there, both Customs Agents. So I think to myself ... we're dead.

At this point the Customs lady poked her head through the window. "Do you have anything to declare?"

"Well, we did try to camp, but that didn't work out. You can tell by the blankets in the back," I told her.

"What's the most expensive thing you bought?"

I thought about that one for a minute because it wasn't me that bought the chair. "I think it was these two frying pans."

"How much were they?"

"About forty-five bucks."

She said, "O.K.," then she turned to Elaine. "And what did you buy?"

By now Elaine was petrified. She turned her head slowly and looked at the wall of clothes behind her. We were sitting ramrod straight with both seats pushed as far ahead as possible to make room for everything in the back. Then she looked at the agent and motioned with her head to the back. "I think probably the chair in there."

The agent looked surprised. "There's a chair back there? What type of chair is it?"

"Well, it's a leather chair. It's to help my back. I get back spasms."

"A leather chair?"

"Yeah."

"How much did you pay for the chair?"

"I don't remember."

"Do you have a receipt? What does it say?"

Elaine began searching for the receipt that she'd just written out. "It says $500.00 dollars."

"Is that in U.S. or Canadian?"

"I don't know, it doesn't say."

I turned and looked at her. "Elaine, you know it's gotta be five hundred bucks in American." So I said to the agent, "We've driven a long way, she's very tired."

'Does that include tax?"

Elaine peered at the receipt. "No, there's no tax. Actually, I can't read the writing."

"Ladies, would you like to pull over there?" The woman pointed to a space on the side because obviously we were going to have to go inside to write out a declaration. And again I thought to myself ... oh, oh, we're dead! But what could I do? So I pulled over.

She looked into the P.T. Cruiser, "Do you want to haul that chair out for me?"

So I opened the door at the back and all the stuff we'd crammed in fell out at her feet. She took one look at it and she could see that a lot of it was small odds and ends and not impressive at all. So she said, "I'll tell you what, come inside. Have you got your receipts? "

Although I'd pitched out most of mine somewhere in Utah, I told her, "Yeah, we've got our receipts. Well, that is, some of them."

We went in with Elaine crying. "Oh, I'm so sorry, I've never bought that much before, so I've never had to pay."

By sheer luck Elaine happened to get one of the nicest agents who told her, "Well, the chair can be in a different category ... especially if it's for your back." By the time she'd finished, Elaine only doled out $35.00.

We got back into the car, with Elaine much relieved and happy to get going home.

The Visa came next month. Ted was very much surprised when he saw that the price of the chair in Canadian money was $2,000.00.

Elaine looked shocked. "I didn't know it cost that much Canadian! I'll be much more careful next time. Trust me! I really will!"

Ted just looked dumbfounded! But he paid the bill and let it pass.

THE END

EASTER CANDY

My mother always had a different philosophy about life. She often said, "Always deal with things straight on." And she stuck with that. Now when my daughter Christina was about five, she had this insatiable sweet tooth. She loved candy so much, if she could find it, she would steal it. And if I left anything sweet in the house, somehow she always managed to sniff it out. Christmas, she'd look for boxes of chocolate under the tree, then she'd open them and eat them in her room.

Christina was a chocoholic right from the start. I kept complaining to my mother, "Mom, when this girl grows up, she's going to weigh 200 pounds. What are we going to do with her? I'm sure her face will be all pimples. She's going to be a mess. I never had a sweet tooth like her. This is ridiculous!"

My mom just smiled. "Now Carol, I don't think so."

Our family had a cabin in Pigeon Lake where my mom and dad spent a lot of their free time. The next time they went out there, I got a phone call from Mom.

"You're coming down for Easter, right?"

I sighed. "Great! Mom, you know what'll happen with Christina, don't you? Yeah, she'll be on a sugar high for at least five days. You'll see, it'll be just awful."

"You know what? I think I've got a solution."

"What is it?"

"Wait and see."

I was more than willing. "Okay."

So when I, Scott, my husband, Christina, and our son Kelly, decided to spend Easter with my folks at the lake, my mom and I went shopping for Easter goodies.

I dreaded it, because I knew what Christina would be like when she saw what we'd bought. I never worried about Kelly, he didn't seem to care for the candy. But with Christina, she went absolutely nuts about anything sweet.

We stopped at the local grocery store and my mom pointed to some chocolates. "Carol, we'll buy the cheapest, crappiest candy we can find. You see those chocolate marshmallow things?"

"What about them?"

"We'll buy lots of those.'

"You see that Allen's chocolate over there ... that really sweet kind?"

"Yeah."

"We'll buy lots of Allen's."

So we went through the candy and bought some of nearly every variety.

My mom was quite satisfied with what we'd picked and said to me, "You just watch me."

Once home, she did this Easter egg hunt thing for the kids and hid all the gooey stuff all over the house. There was chocolate everywhere you turned, and she didn't make it hard to find.

Christina thought she'd died and gone to heaven. My mom surprised her with one those huge chocolate Easter bunnies, several cream filled Easter eggs, as well as other varieties of chocolate... most of which was sickly sweet.

Anyway, we got it all hidden. Christina, as soon as she found it, true to her nature, started bolting it down saying, "Well that's what Easter is all about, isn't it?"

Every time I looked at her she was chowing down on some kind of candy. Then she started going to town on the chocolate.

My mom, who's really cool, said to her, "You really like chocolate, don't you, dear?"

Though her mouth was full, she managed to say, "Mm-mm-mm, yeah, I luv chocolate."

"Christina, I'll make a deal with you. Do you want to eat dinner tonight?"

"Hm-m-m, no, actually I'm full. I don't need any dinner."

"I'll tell you what. I'll let you go on a chocolate diet. You don't have to eat real food anymore. You can just eat chocolate. We'll show your mother what you really like to eat, okay?"

Christina's eyes lit up. She was just the happiest camper! She sidled up to me to brag, "Ha, ha, Grandma's on my side. She said I can have all the candy I want."

"Is that right? Okay." I looked at my mom, wondering what her strategy was.

She just said, "Run with it."

Well, that evening my mom made steak, baked potatoes and corn on the cob for the rest of us. It was a fabulous meal. But for Christina, she decorated a plate with an assortment of chocolate, marshmallows and candy. And she really did a great job on the decorating.

Christina sat down with a big smile on her face, as if to say, "Look at what you're missing, and me, I get all this."

She savored every bite. I never saw anybody look happier in my life.

When she finished, my mom asked her, "Would you like a snack now, dear? Would you like another chocolate?"

Christina's eyes lit up. "Oh, yes, I'd like another chocolate."

She went off to bed soon after. She tossed and turned for a while before falling asleep.

The next day when she woke up, we had our usual bacon and egg breakfast. However for Christina, Mom plunked down another plateful of chocolate delight. There was every variety of chocolate you can imagine. Christina ate all of it, then went off to do her own thing.

At lunch we all had grilled cheese sandwiches, except for Christina. She had chocolate, chocolate, chocolate!

Something told me that she was starting to slow down. She looked at everybody's plate, then at hers. However, being very stubborn, she was still not ready to give up.

That evening my mom went out and brought home Kentucky fried chicken, which happened to be one of Christina's favorite foods, as well as mashed potatoes, gravy and corn muffins. You can't get much better than that.

We sat down and ate this delicious chicken. The smell went right through the house. Meanwhile, Christina sat eating her chocolates one more time. For two and a half days she'd had nothing but chocolate and candy.

About dinner on the third day, she came up to my mom and said, "Grandma, I have a tummy ache."

I thought she might have had the tummy ache for the last forty eight hours, but being stubborn she wouldn't admit it.

Then I heard her say, "Grandma, do you have something to eat?"

"Oh, that's no problem, you still have lots of your chocolate left. I'll take you to the back room where I have all your goodies. And in fact, I'll let you pick out your own plate."

"Grandma, I don't think I feel good enough to do that."

"No? Well come with me anyway. I want to show you some things you haven't even tried yet."

So my mom pulled her into the back room.

Christina literally turned green when she saw the candy. Very quickly she ran for the bathroom. She was out in about five minutes.

My mom didn't say anything but she gave me a "don't rub it in" look.

We walked back into the dining room and sat down for dinner.

Once more Mom made another of Christina's favorites... hamburger and fries. We were all sitting down when Christina pulled my mom aside to whisper, "Don't tell anybody, but I want one of those. I want some real food. Don't tell Mom I said that."

My mom nodded and winked at me, as she filled her plate with "real food." And from that day on, Christina never again felt the same about chocolate. She totally lost her love for it, and to this day she doesn't crave it anymore.

THE END

THE MUFFIN SNACK

Once upon a time when my daughter, Christina, was in grade two, it seemed that I was always behind the eight ball, always forgetting things and always being reminded to do things. This particular night I came home after work from the car wash about 9:00, and Christina reminded me that I had to make muffins for all the kids and her teacher. It was my turn and my responsibility once a month to provide a snack.

I thought about doing the muffins right away, but we'd had a very busy day at the car wash and I was dead tired. So rather than baking them that evening, I planned to get up early, so the kids would have nice hot muffins to take to school in the morning. I decided to make orange muffins, which requires putting some oranges into the blender and blending them with flour, sugar, butter etc.

I calculated that since both my children were picked up by a school bus in front of our house, and they usually left at a quarter to eight, I could easily get up about 6:00 or 6;15

and it would give me enough time to mix them, bake them, and put them into a bag. It's a great idea, I thought.

A problem occurred when I didn't get up until 7:00. We lived on an acreage and I knew there wasn't enough time to pick up some ready made muffins from a bakery and have them ready in time for the kids to take with them on the bus.

So I thought, I just better do the best I can. I got out the oranges, put them into my Cuisinart processer, ground them up, added the eggs, then went to get the flour. Suddenly, I discovered that I only had a half a cup of flour left and the recipe called for two and a half cups.

I almost gave up, thinking that unfortunately the orange muffins weren't going to happen today. Then at the last minute I found that I had on hand a Robin Hood bran muffin mix ... a brand that I'd never tried before, but I'd bought it because it was cheap and I thought, you know it might work.

I ended up putting in the mix and then adding some raisins to it. I didn't have any chocolate chips to put in and I really felt bad about that because I thought the kids would have liked chips. The other problem was that after I threw the entire mix into the blender, it occurred to me that it only made 24 muffins and I had calculated that I needed at least thirty.

So what could a person do? Why not throw in the half cup of flour and add some more water. In my rush, I forgot to put in the sugar. Still hoping for the best, I added a couple more teaspoons of baking soda thinking to make it rise a little bit higher. Anyway, I left it at that. At this point things still weren't at crisis level because it was only ten after seven and I thought I'd still have maybe thirty minutes to bake the muffins.

The next problem occurred when I went to get the tins out to cook the muffins in. I only had two pans which made twenty-four muffins. I was still six short.

I must remind you that since I didn't have my coffee that morning, my artistic ability to make it all work still hadn't kicked in.

I found a cake tin and lined it with foil, then I bunched the foil up at one end and poured in just enough batter to what I thought would make six muffins. I planned to slice them into squares. Now I didn't check to see how long it would take to bake the bran muffins because my orange muffins only took twenty-five minutes. And all the time I was thinking that this is gonna work because I still have time. However, I happened to glance at the box only to note that the bran muffins took forty-five minutes to bake.

Now I'm short of time. So I thought why not turn up the oven to make them cook faster. The oven temperature for the mix was supposed to be 350 degrees, but I turned it up to 450. At this point, I have to admit that turning up the temperature was not such a good idea especially when I left the oven grate at the very bottom of the stove. But with the heat up, I figured they should be done in thirty minutes instead of forty-five.

In the meantime, I was wildly running around trying to get my two children ready for school. Anyway, I totally forgot about the muffins until Christina shouted out, "Mom, can you smell something burning? Mom, I think the muffins are burning!"

So I rushed to the stove and turned the light on inside. And yes, they did look kind of burnt, but it's only around the edges and it can't be all that bad, I told myself. So I continued to let them bake, but I did turn the temperature right down ... at the same time hoping the bus would be late.

Suddenly Christina yelled out, "Mom, Mom, I think the bus is coming down our road! It's coming into our yard! ... Mom, Mom, you know the bus won't wait for us!"

I said, "No problem. I'll get these out right away." I remembered too late that I forgot to grease the tinfoil and now they're stuck tight to the tinfoil. But I was still not convinced that they wouldn't come out. So I grabbed a spatula and scraped them out then proceeded to cut them, keeping my eyes shut to the fact that they might still be raw.

At this point panic seized me. "Christina quick, I need a plastic bag!"

She produced a Safeway shopping bag. I literally threw the muffins into the bag still steaming hot.

Meanwhile, Kelly, my son, was at the door yelling, "Mom, Mom, the bus is waiting! Hurry! Quick, it's about to leave!"

Christina grabbed the bag and started running for the door. Suddenly, I heard a plop, plop, plop on the floor. She stopped to yell, "Mom! Mom! The bag is melting!"

To my horror, the muffins were so hot they had melted the plastic bag and were rolling on the floor. But I thought, I did wash the floor and they shouldn't be too bad. So at that point, I did what any normal mom would do, I found a paper bag and picked them up and threw them into the bag.

"Hurry, Mom!" Christina grabbed the bag and went running for the bus.

I tried very hard to put the entire fiasco out of my mind for the entire whole day.

But it took three days before I had the nerve to ask my daughter how my muffins had been received. I hoped against all hope that they tasted better than they looked because they were burnt at the top, they were falling apart, and the one's I'd cut into six were in pieces ... not necessarily a square, and I'd forgotten to add the sugar.

Christina looked at me somberly and said, "Mom, I don't want to hurt your feelings, but the kids said that they were the worst muffins they'd ever tasted in their entire life, and the teacher told me to tell you... and Mom, I don't know how to tell you this without hurting your feelings, but she doesn't want you to bake anything anymore, anytime, for any reason. In fact, you don't have to make anything for the rest of the year, Miss Raymond said this."

"Well, I'd just like to know what shape they were in? Were they squished?"

"Squished? Well no, not exactly. When we opened the bag they were still steaming and they were all melted at the bottom. They looked like glue!"

"Oh! Well actually, I'm not surprised. Sorry, I can't believe that I did that. Maybe next time I'll do better."

"No, Mom, no next time, you don't have to make anything anymore. Miss Raymond made that very clear."

THE END

THE TOUCHLESS CAR WASH

My Dad and I run a car wash. Last year my Dad went to a Car Wash convention in Las Vegas. While there he stopped at one of the displays to look at some Touchless Car Wash equipment. As soon as the fellow in the booth noticed his interest, he came out to talk to him. My Dad casually mentioned that he was from Edmonton, Alberta.

The salesman looked quite interested. "Oh, you might like to know that we installed this very same equipment in Alberta about a year ago. Actually, in quite a thriving community."

"Oh yeah? Where might that be ... Calgary, Edmonton, or maybe Lethbridge?"

The young man shook his head. "No, it was Vegreville."

"Vegreville? You don't say!" My Dad looked at him kind of skeptical. The population there is about 5,000, or less. Now you have to understand that this equipment is about $200,000.00 U.S., plus there would be the cost of the building, the land, and the operating cost. Quite an undertaking to make it pay in a small town such as Vegreville.

As soon as my Dad returned home, he was somewhat curious as to how well the "touchless car wash" was doing and if it paid well.

One morning I was in the office catching up on the paperwork when he popped in on me.

"Carol, I've gotta see that car wash in action. You know the one I told you about? I thought today might be a good day ... bright, sunny, shame to waste it in here ... don't you think? I think I'll take a drive to Vegreville. I'd like to see how that machinery works and if it does a good job. If I like it, I'll consider getting one for us."

My Dad got there around 3;00 o'clock. He noticed it was a car wash that stood alone because there was nobody running it. Just a sign that told you step by step how to get through the wash. So he sat there and waited about 25 minutes for someone to show up. At this point there was not a soul around, but he was determined to see a demonstration, so he waited. There would be no use in cleaning his own car because it was clean.

Finally he saw a truck, one lone truck coming over the hill into town. It was a woman with an older truck. She pulled up to the car wash, but she didn't pull up quite far enough to the wicket.

There is a beam and once you drive across that beam, a computer system comes on which tells you what to do, but because she hadn't crossed that beam, she didn't know what to do.

My Dad, after sitting and watching her for about 5 minutes, decided to get out of the car and walk over to her.

"Ma'am, if you want your car washed, you'll have to pull up a little further for the machine to come on. A computer screen will tell you what to do. All you have to do is read it and follow the instructions."

She smiled. "Oh, that's great, thank you very much."

So she pulled up a little further. All of a sudden, a screen lit up. It read, "Welcome to Sudsy Car Wash!"

"Ma'am, now you have a choice. What type of a car wash do you want? Exterior, or exterior with wax, or underblast ... or whatever else. They have the prices marked on the side."

So she sat there, hesitating and just kept looking at the screen, not understanding exactly what it meant because all she really wanted was a "simple car wash."

Again my Dad walked up to her because she was still sitting there and just looking at the screen.

"Ma'am, do you want, just a car wash?"

"Yes, that's all I want, just a car wash."

"Well, that's $7.00."

"Yes, okay." Again she sat there looking at the screen.

"Uh-h-h, ma'am, you have to put the money into the machine. You can use either a credit card or cash to put into the machine."

She looked at him, puzzled. "But how is that machine going to know?"

"To know? You see that slot there? That one is for the credit card and the slot down below, the one with the picture of a bill beside it, that's for the money."

"But how is it going to know what size bill I put in?"

"That's because it has a computer inside and it's going to be able to read how much that bill is."

"But where will I get the change because all I have is a ten dollar bill?"

"Down at the bottom, you'll get your change."

She said, "Okay."

She took out a ten dollar bill and put it into the machine with great difficulty because she put it in the wrong way, just the same as the rest of us would do. So my Dad turned it the right way and got it into the machine and out plunked $3.00 in change.

She got back into the truck and a sign lit up that said, 'Thank you very much for coming in. Now proceed ahead to the first Stop Sign.'

A door opened up in front of her and she started to drive ahead.

Though she drove forward, she didn't notice the next stop sign. Instead, she went all the way through the car wash to the blow dryer area with an unwashed truck.

At this point, my Dad had taken a position at the back of the car wash because he was anxious to see it in action. But when he saw what happened, he walked through the car wash to tell the lady what to do next.

"Ma'am, you'll have to back up because now you've actually gone too far." He was still determined to see how it worked.

"Ma'am, there's a sign board back there, and you stop at that sign board, and you religiously watch it, and you don't move until it tells you to move."

So the lady backed up the truck and just sat there with her eyes glued to the signboard and she didn't move until the water gushed out. However, it barely wet the truck because now she'd backed up too far.

But she kept sitting until the screen read, 'Pull ahead.' So she pulled right ahead. Then, though the blowers came on, she missed that part as well, because she went a little past the blowers.

At this point, the truck was only partly clean and still soaking wet. However, she proceeded to the outside door because a sign came up that told her to "Drive Ahead."

When the outside door opened, my Dad just stood there shaking his head. He watched as she pulled out of the car wash, but not quite far enough so that the back end of the truck was still partly inside the building.

The lady rolled down the window to thank my Dad for all his help, though the truck was not at all clean.

So my Dad said to her, "Well, you know, you could have gotten it blown off a little better, maybe even washed."

All of a sudden the door, which is an automatic door, sensed that the truck was no longer inside and started to come down because the bumper, though it had crossed the line where the door came down, hadn't crossed the sensor to indicate that the truck was still partially inside. The door hit the back of the bumper and now sat angled on the bumper because it couldn't go down all the way.

My Dad looked up and he could see that the cables that hold this door are on rollers and they've slipped off completely and are now going Zing! Zing! Zing! round and round and round. "Oh, my God!" was all he said.

The lady looked behind when she heard the noise. Suddenly, she panicked, put the truck into gear and whizzed off at a terrific rate of speed. Meanwhile, as soon as the door slid off the bumper, it whomped down with one resounding thud.

By now all the cables had flown off and the door was hanging at a dangerous slant and there was no way that it would work if anybody should come along to wash their car.

My Dad examined the damaged door. Then he noticed a sign beside the door. 'In an emergency call Hank at 232-4222.'

I wonder how often this is used? he thought. At $7.00 a wash per hour, if the car wash is open ten hours a day, on a sunny day it would reap $70.00. He calculated that Hank's total investment would take him years to pay off. Not much of an investment.

He knew that the next guy who came in to use the car wash wouldn't know that the back door was broken. So he did the only decent thing, he phoned the owner and explained how the lady had pulled up, didn't understand the operations of such a sophisticated car wash, and had wrecked the door.

What he didn't tell him was that he'd witnessed the whole thing. But since the poor man was only making $70.00 a day, he didn't want to ruin his day any further. My Dad figured that his best bet would be to move the car wash to the city where he could pay off the cost in double quick time.

THE END

THE LOST LUGGAGE

This is a story of traveling on the airlines of today. The airlines of yesterday were actually a treat, you got meals, drinks, champagne for breakfast if you happened to be traveling that early, and almost anything else you wanted. Today everything is booked on line.

My husband Scott and I live in Edmonton, Alberta. And for investment purposes, we bought a house several miles outside of Orlando, Florida. Occasionally, we go there to check on it. Since we had done some renovations to the property by phone and email, we decided to fly to Florida in late February. It was still very cold in Edmonton and I knew Orlando would be warm.

My dad would be looking after the car wash while we were gone so that wasn't a problem. I manage a car wash which my Dad owns. Scott and I have two children. Christina is now married and Kelly lives on his own and is about to be married. So Scott and I were quite free to travel.

Of course I haven't had a lot of experience booking on line, but I booked a trip on line to Florida. From Edmonton it wasn't a direct flight. We had a choice of going to Orlando, on several different routes. So like everybody else, I always look at the price first and check to see how long it's going to take us to get there.

I never worried about the connections, or anything else and I never really thought about the time it took to make those connections between flights.

So we flew from Edmonton to Chicago and we found out that we had only fifty minutes to catch a plane from Chicago to Florida.

Now if anyone knows the Chicago airport, they know that it's virtually impossible to catch another flight in fifty minutes from Chicago. Actually, the fact of the matter is that when the plane left the ground in Edmonton, the crew had to d-ice it first, which took like thirty minutes. So we were late coming into Chicago by thirty minutes.

So when we landed in Chicago, there was no one to greet us or tell us you which direction to go, or where to find a map. They only give you a map of the terminal where you get off.

About that time, we realized that we weren't even in the right terminal. So we go down and find some guy who looks like he's with the airport and I said to him, "We need to find terminal "C."

"Well," he says, "you need to go down the stairs. There should be a shuttle there, and it'll take you right across the tarmac to terminal C."

At this point, I think we had like 10 minutes to catch our plane. So Scott and I run down the stairs and the shuttle bus is just filling up and there's no real sitting room left.

So I say to the attendant, "We have to make this flight."

And the attendant says, "Well ma,am, there'll be another shuttle right away. This one is full."

The fact of the matter is that there is no other shuttle bus right away because this same shuttle bus has to go to the other terminal and unload first, then reload the passengers coming from that terminal and bring them back to this terminal where we're waiting. Well, by the time the shuttle got back it was time for our plane to leave.

At that point, I think you know there's really not much hope of making that plane unless that plane is really late. But as luck would have it, we get up there and I can see the plane still waiting outside the door. But by now I look down the hallway and I see the doors are already shut to the ramp.

I look outside and it's about 20 degrees below in Chicago, snowing and really horrible and I'm thinking to myself that we really don't want to get stuck in Chicago.

So I said to the girl at the counter, "It's very imperative we get to Florida today."

And the girl says, "Well, unfortunately, I don't know if your bags will make that plane."

And I'm thinking, I know there's no way the bags will make the plane in 20 minutes. "It's not a problem about the bags, we have to catch this plane," I tell her.

And at that point, I noticed that she was already selling our tickets to someone else in line because we hadn't shown up in time.

So she stopped what she was doing when she saw us and she told someone in charge, "Open that door and let them go in."

Well, when we got on the plane, we got the most meanest looks from the passengers. But we sat down and finally we landed in Orlando. Our bags did show up the next day.

Unfortunately, our flight back had the same connections except that we had one extra connection. We had to go through North Carolina and that's where the story begins.

We were to fly from Florida at 12:00 noon. And it was a bad day because we got lost on our way to the airport and we barely made the flight. Anyway, when we finally got on the plane, we had an hour and ten minutes in North Carolina, and we had to take the North Carolina flight to Chicago and change planes in Chicago to get back to Edmonton.

We got on the plane in North Carolina and once again the plane is late leaving North Carolina for Chicago.

We get into the Chicago airport and it's probably once more about 10 or 15 minutes that we have to catch the next plane back to Edmonton. And this time I'm sure that we won't be lucky enough to make it.

Anyway, we hurry. Scott takes off ahead of me and he's running full force with suitcase in hand and I'm struggling behind him and I can't really run pulling a suitcase. But he's going to try to make the plane to get us on. I'm coming behind him as fast as I can until one of those gals with a cart comes along. So I say, "Excuse me, excuse me, miss, can I get a lift?" So she gives me a ride.

I can see Scott, he's like ten feet ahead of me and still running. Then I see this gal, who's wandering through the airport, a passenger from one of the planes that have just come in, and she stops the gal who's driving our cart to ask, "Do you know where I can buy a suit at this airport?" Then she goes into fine detail about what kind of suit she wants. So I'm listening to her story and thinking, now for sure we'll never make it.

The lady driving the cart listens to her then says. "Well, you know ... blah, blah blah!" So for 10 or 15 minutes she hemmed and hawed about where and how to buy the suit. She made about three phone calls on her cell, keeping us waiting on the cart.

So finally I said, "I'm sorry I have to do this. Could you just ... I don't know how much further I have to go, but could you just tell her that you have to give me a ride to the terminal because as of now I'm late? And then maybe come back and tell her where she can buy the suit?" So she started up the cart and took us the rest of the way.

By this time Scott's up there and they're already telling him the doors are shut and they're saying, "I'm sorry, but our policy is unless your bags are with you when you're making the flight, we can't let you get on the plane."

I'm not a crying person. But I started to put on a crying act. I'm doing my best to bawl, which doesn't come easy, so I say, "I'm sorry but my animals are being dropped off at my house today and there's no one to look after them and it's 30 below outside. Now I've got to get home to take care of them, or they'll freeze to death. You don't want them to freeze, do you?"

I don't know if she realized that my pets being inside, when it was 30 below outside, didn't have any bearing on freezing to death because they were quite safe. But being the fact that she was from the States, she maybe thought I lived in an igloo.

She must have had pets of her own because she felt quite sympathetic towards me. So she got hold of her manager. "Yes, I know," she says. "She's okay that her bags won't be coming with her."

"Have they closed the door to the inside of the plane?" the manager wants to know.

"No, they haven't done that."

"Well, on this occasion, we'll let her get on."

Well, Scott and I felt quite smart with ourselves that we actually got on that plane. But you have to have a thick skin because again everybody was giving us really dirty looks for being late.

So finally we get back to Edmonton and I didn't even bother waiting for our bags to go around that carousel, or check for them, because I knew that there was no way the bags would have made it.

So I go in to make a report of the type of bags we have, our flight number, and the number of bags.

"There'll be a flight tomorrow. They should arrive tomorrow, and after they clear customs, we'll give you a call," the girl at the check-in counter says to me.

The next day comes and goes and I haven't heard anything. Well, we'll give it one more day I think. They have to go through customs and everything else. If I drive down now I'll be just wasting my time. But they did give me a tracking number because I had to fill out two official forms with tracking numbers because Scott had a suitcase and I had a suitcase. So I phoned the day after that because I still hadn't seen the suitcases. Now we're up to day three.

On the third day, I phoned the airline and got a voice message. "If you have a claim number, type the claim number into the phone and we'll tell you currently where your bags are."

So I did that and they said they were in Edmonton. Okay. So I phoned another number and I asked, "When can I come and pick them up."

"Well, no, not yet. They have to go through customs."

"So how long do you expect that to take?"

"It can be anywhere from twelve hours to thirty-eight hours."

In other words, they don't know. So I said, "That's fine, I can live without my suitcase for another couple of days."

Now we enter the fifth day and I still haven't heard anything. So I phoned over there and the girl checks the tracking number and she says, "I don't know where they are."

"Well, they said they were in Edmonton. They were going through customs."

She said, "For all intents and purposes this tracking number has been eliminated from our system. Every five days we eliminate all tracking numbers. So I will suggest that you come in and fill out a baggage claim report."

So I said, "Well, what do you mean by that?"

"A lost baggage report."

"But they're not lost. They're there ... at the airport."

She says, "As far as we're concerned they're lost. So put in your claim and if they don't show up we can send you a check for $200.00."

"What's the two hundred for?"

"Well, that's our policy. We'll give you $200.00."

"But my suitcase and the contents are worth much more than that."

"Well, that's what we're insured for and that's all you get."

"Well, you know what? The suitcase is there. At the airport. I just want it back. Just let me get to it."

"Well, I guess you can come down and have a look at our lost baggage department and see if you can find it."

"Well I will do that."

So I went the next day and I got there at 4:15 in the afternoon.

"You want the baggage claim lady? Oh, sorry, you missed her by 15 minutes. She quits work at 4:00."

"Well what time does she start work?"

"Well, it varies from day to day. Maybe eight o'clock, maybe nine, depending when the flights come in."

"Can I get a phone number and see when she's going to be in?"

"Oh, I'm sorry, we can't give out the phone number for the baggage department. You'll have to call a 1-800 number in the United States and they'll contact us about it."

"So where is this magical office?"

"It's actually behind me about five feet."

"Gee, can I go back there and can I just maybe have a look?"

"I can't let you do that. I can't leave my post. But I really sympathize with you."

"But I just paid $4.00 for parking outside."

"I'm really sorry but there's nothing I can do. Come back again when you can."

So the next day I come back again. I come back at 3:30. And the same gal is at the front check-in.

"I'm here to talk to the baggage handler."

"I don't know how to tell you this today, but the flight was canceled and we sent the baggage handler home early."

"I notice that you said, "the baggage handler." Do you only have one?"

"Yes."

If you ever wonder why it takes so long to get your baggage off the plane, it's because they've got only one person doing the job.

"Well surely somebody else besides her can look for the luggage."

"Well, this is your lucky day. Because there's nobody here and nobody's checking in, I can go behind the counter with you and we can take a quick look inside and see if you can spot your luggage."

So I go around the counter and to a room that is about 8 feet by 8 feet. This is their baggage room. Pretty small. And it's pretty easy to see if the bag is there or not. So I looked around the room, but my bag was not in there.

Now I must tell you that earlier that morning, I got a bag delivered to the car wash. Well, anyway, one of the two that were lost. So I asked the fellow who delivered it, "Where is my other bag?"

"I have no idea. We only had the one bag to deliver."

The next day, again I strike off to the airport in search of my luggage. Well at least now I know for sure that both bags must have been there at some point. I went to the same lady as before.

"Where is my bag? You delivered my husband's suitcase yesterday. So where's mine?"

"Sorry, it's not here. There's nothing I can do. You'll have to come back tomorrow."

"Is there any point?"

"It could still be in Customs."

"Seven days later? ... You know I'm up to $12.00 for parking. It's $4.00 for twenty minutes ... I got my one bag. I just need my other one."

"I don't know how to tell you this, but the baggage clerk is not in the back room right now."

"Is she out for a coffee break ... lunch?"

"I don't know where she is, ma'am."

"Can't you page her?"

"I can't page her in the International Airport just looking for her. I'm sorry it doesn't work that way."

"Fine. Then I'm prepared to wait. I can't make another trip and that's final."

So I'm sitting waiting for this gal. And I see the check-in lady on her cell phone and I hear her say, "Well, she's not giving up. She's sitting and waiting."

So this tells me that she must have been able to contact her because she has a cellphone, no doubt. Well, pretty soon the baggage clerk shows up and she takes me to the original room that I looked into just a few days ago. That was yesterday, or maybe the day before and I didn't see my bag then and I don't see it now.

So she says, "We have one other little room, it's on the main floor, that we could go look in. I'll walk you down there and we'll have a look."

The room is where all the International flights come in. And it's right beside "Customs." So she takes me into this locked area. It's a room about 8 feet by 10. And in this room there had to be at least a hundred suitcases. And lo and behold, as I looked around that room, I noticed some of the suitcases had dust on the labels, they'd been there that long. And these labels have names and addresses and phone numbers on them. And nobody's contacting anybody. So as I looked around that room ... to my surprise, there was my suitcase!

"There it is!" I said to her.

"Well, aren't you lucky!" she says.

Apparently this is what happens. After all the different suitcases from all the different airlines go through customs, and if it happens that there's no one to claim them, they're put into this "dead room." I'll call it the "dead room" because nothing moves from the "dead room."

"Now what's supposed to happen is that all the different airlines, from time to time, have to go into that room to check and see if any of their lost suitcases are in there. Now you've got to remember that there's only one baggage handler clerk, and the clerk isn't going to go down daily to see if a missing suitcase can be found. And you won't get a phone number directly, so that you can check.

They delete your lost baggage out of the system in five days, so as far as they're concerned it's "dead." So I would think if you're ever short of a suitcase after a trip, you might want to check in the "dead room." Every airport has one. So don't give up! Your missing suitcase is in there, you may be sure. Be persistent just as I was!

THE END

THE MORNING AFTER

When I was dating, oh, at about the age of twenty, I had a very active social life. Just like my friend, Maria, I had more boyfriends than I could count. We were good girls, and we did have a lot of fun. There were night clubs and there were discos, but the problem was that the discos would go on till one in the morning and we had to work the next day. At that particular point in my life I had actually met my husband, Scott, though he wasn't my husband at the time and I was still dating Howard.

On this one particular date, I had had a late night because we'd gone out for dinner and dancing and I didn't get home until one o'clock. I was dead dog tired. As soon as I got in, I took off my pant suit and I went to bed. Of course I was late getting up in the morning and because of my social life, I was really bad about getting all my laundry done. So what would a normal person do? They'd grab what they wore the night before. After all, I'd only worn that pantsuit once, so it should still be okay, I thought.

By now I was running really late, so I quickly put on my underwear and my pantsuit, then I proceeded to go to work. I worked for the Federal Government as an office clerk. Though I was really tired that day, I decided to walk downtown to the Eaton's Centre and have lunch.

As I got out of the building, this nice good-looking young man tapped me on the shoulder from behind. "Uh-h-h, miss, I think you're losing something."

Now you could take that remark 'you're losing something' in many, many ways.

So I stopped then and there and I wondered exactly what he was referring to? Since I've done this before, I looked down at my feet to see if I had the same shoes on, because one day I left the house with a brown shoe and a green shoe. No, they checked out. I looked to see if I had a shirt on? Yes, that's very important. Then I looked to see if I had my pants on and if they were done up. They were. So I proceeded to take total inventory of myself and I thought what else could there be?

Again he pointed to me and he said, "Actually, you're dragging something."

And I said, "I'm dragging something?"

"Yes!" and he pointed down.

I looked down.

He said, "No, behind you."

So I looked behind me.

He said, "Down there!"

So I looked down to where he was pointing, and for about a foot and a half I could see my pantyhose on the ground. They were attached to my pantleg on the inside and I was walking down Jasper Avenue with my pantyhose trailing behind. I had worn them like that all morning. Right? At that point, I was fairly slim and I had lots of room in my pants, so it could happen. So I wondered what am I going to do? There's like a thousand people behind me. How am I going to pull my panyhose out and shove them out of sight?

I saw an alcove close by. Of course they were the leotard type of pantyhose and they were stuck in the crotch somewhere. I tried, but it was too hard to pull them off. And there was no graceful way of doing this. After pulling and pulling, I gave up. Then I remembered that I had a pair of scissors in my purse. So I cut them off at the bottom of my pant leg and casually started back to the office. I looked around for the young man who'd alerted me, wanting to thank him, but he was no longer in sight. I silently thanked him wondering how long they'd been dragging behind me and why no one at work noticed or told me about it.

THE END

THE ELVIS PRESLEY SANDWICH

Barbara and Grant Foster had just bought a new show home in Terrace Gardens … an attractive duplex condo. They moved in. Barbara was quite satisfied with the Condo. It was a lovely home. After they'd unpacked and put all into place, she thought it would be nice to have some of her family, she had five boys all married, over for dinner at some time because the house was quite spacious and could easily accommodate at least 20 people.

The next day, she heard Grant organizing the garage which was okay with her because it meant that she didn't have to do it. It was getting close to lunch and she thought about making him something to eat.

"Barbara, what's for lunch?" he soon called out.

"Uh-h-h, I'll get something ready," she assured him, not really positive about what it would be. Then she remembered the "Elvis Presley" sandwich. She'd seen the recipe on television. It was something she could put together in a hurry and Grant did like peanut butter.

She made the sandwich and called him inside.

"Good choice, Barbara. I like it."

After lunch she decided to call her cousin, Rachael. She hadn't heard from Rachael since they'd moved. Rachael often called her about recipes.

"Rachael! So how are you? Just finished lunch. I made Grant a sandwich, an Elvis Presley sandwich."

"You what? What kind of sandwich did you say? Elvis Presley? Never heard of it. What is it? What's the recipe?"

"Actually, it's quite easy to put together. You start off with a couple of pieces of bread, as you would for any sandwich. So I butter the bread, then I'll spread a couple tablespoons of peanut butter over both pieces. After that, drizzle some honey over the peanut butter, or sprinkle some sugar on it if you don't have any honey. It's simple and takes me but a minute. Then peel a banana and lay it over the bread. Then butter both pieces on the outside and fry it in a frying pan . Remember I said fry both sides. I know now why Elvis liked it so much. It's very rich and quite delicious."

"Barbara, I'm going to make myself that sandwich for lunch. It sounds so good I can't wait to try it."

Barbara put down the phone thinking, she can't possibly mess this one up. It's too easy. She checked on a pot of borscht simmering on the stove. She remembered having given Rachael the recipe for the soup and Rachael did mess it up. The soup was mainly beets and vegetables with a tablespoon of vinegar and about a tablespoon of sugar added to enhance the sweetness of the beets. A day later, she'd phoned her wondering how the soup had turned out.

"Barbara, it was so very good. I added a cup of sugar to it just like you said."

"Rachael, a cup of sugar did you say? A whole cup of sugar?" Really Rachael, I said a tablespoon, no more than that, just a tablespoon. What did it taste like? It's supposed to be soup, Rachael, not beet preserves!"

"But it tasted really good. My Jim, he loved it."

"Well, I never heard of such a thing! Rachael, really, that's far too much sugar to put into soup."

Barbara thought that for some reason Rachael did not have a feel for cooking. Now what will she do to the Elvis Presley sandwich?

She heard from Rachael several days later.

"So how about that Elvis Presley sandwich? Did you like it?"

"Mm-m-m, I'm not sure. I did have some trouble with it. I don't think it was as good as yours."

"In what way? It always works for me."

"I did just like you said. I buttered the bread and put the peanut butter on ... and the honey, then the banana. But the banana stuck out and I had trouble frying it. So I pounded the banana, but that didn't work. I even tried rolling it with a rolling pin. The bread gummed up and the banana got smashed. What do you do with the banana? The bread doesn't wrap around it too good. How do you toast it with the banana sticking out on both sides ?"

"You rolled it? Rachael, do you mean to say that you didn't slice it but you put the whole thing in without slicing it?"

"Yeah, and it stuck out on both sides, like I said... Are you supposed to slice it?"

"Of course you are. How else could you toast it? No wonder it didn't work. I slice mine lengthwise then put it on the bread. Then I fry both sides in butter in a frying pan. Rachael, you've made a grilled cheese sandwich, haven't you? Do it the same way as a grilled cheese."

"Oh Barbara! I had no idea! Thanks for telling me. I'll try it that way."

Barbara shook her head in disbelief. She hung up the phone. Why would Rachael think of pounding it, rolling it, but not slicing it? Some people just don't have a knack for cooking.

THE END

THE TAXI

Anna Moroz checked out the birth certificate for errors, going through it a second time. It would never pass inspection if the computer found even one small mistake. Her job in Vital Statistics, at the Edmonton down town branch, entailed accuracy. Fortunately, she had a penchant for it. Yesterday out of 177 documents that she'd looked through, it pleased her to note that only one had been returned. A small error. She'd missed out the "Fort" from Fort Assiniboine.

All marriage licenses, birth and death certificates, were examined with the same precision for spelling neatness, or anything suspect, giving painstaking care to detail. In the morning she'd run a check on a marriage certificate and found a mistake in the space provided for "birth dates." A Clarence Brown had put down his age as 53, however, his birth date stated that he was actually 60 years old. Sometimes people lied about these things ... to a spouse, boyfriend, or girlfriend, or for whatever reason that one could conjure.

She liked her job. She liked the people she worked with. Most were friendly, meeting her needs when she wanted something.

At noon she went to the coffee room to eat her lunch. Elsa Van Camp and Betty Rourke from her department were already there.

She poured herself some coffee and sat down. "Girls, I need help or perhaps advice. Uh-h-h, I've got some holidays coming and I've got to use them up by the end of this year, or I'll lose them." She smiled. "I was thinking that Anton and I should go to New York. We've never been there. Have you ever been there?"

"I have," Elsa remarked. "I'll say one thing, it's not a place for amateurs. I mean when you get there, you just better remember not to look up at the tall buildings because you could easily be a mark for someone. You've got to act as if you belong, as if you know where you're going and not just some gawking tourist."

"Oh really?"

Betty Rourke put down her coffee. "Well, I've never been there, but if you do go remember that you're eligible for the Government Discount. Hotels are quite expensive and it's a saving. Actually, I know of a place that's quite cheap. It's called "The Ollcott." I hear a lot of Canadians stay there. You know Mr. Moore from the Audit department? Well, when he went I typed up a list of all the different hotels he could stay at, their addresses, telephone numbers, even prices."

Anna leaned forward. "Actually, that's just what I want, prices. Could you give me a copy of that list? We can't afford expensive places. Anton's saving for a new car. The old one is about ready to give in."

"Yeah, I guess I could. One more thing, I believe "The Ollcott" is only $50.00 a day Canadian. Just remember to make the reservations as soon as you can."

Anna went back to her desk. She could hardly wait to get home to tell Anton. Would he reject the idea because he'd rather have the car? He was employed at the Lilydale Poultry Plant. He had what she called a "go-for" job. His specialty ... running errands for maintenance, searching out parts in electrical and plumbing to keep the large plant going, in fact the largest in Alberta and Canada. He drove a company truck and the boss kept him busy "going for" one thing and another.

However, since Anna had the run of the house, as well as the marriage pretty much to her liking, she considered Anton to be a good man. That evening she brought up the impending holiday.

"Would you like to try New York?" she asked.

He shrugged. "Anna, why ask me? If that's what you want, then it's okay with me. You know that."

"Yeah, yeah, I know Anton. But you're saving for a new car and I thought you might not want to go. You know, I'd like some of your input. It's your holiday too. And later I don't want to be blamed if something goes wrong and it turns out that you didn't like it. That's why I want both of us to agree on where we go."

He had this quirk about him ... never committing himself on any given issue, leaving it to her, but the rub would come later should she make the wrong decision. Anton could end up angry for several days. However, she knew that he was never a serious threat and soon enough he'd forgive her because he wasn't one to hold a grudge for very long.

He got up from his chair. "Uh-h-h, you decide. I'm going to watch the football game."

"Okay, but remember Anton, I asked you and you didn't exactly say no. Lila can look in on the boys ... in case they need something."

He shrugged. "I wouldn't worry about them if I were you. At sixteen and twenty I'm sure they can look after themselves."

The next evening Anna dropped some travel brochures on the kitchen counter. After supper she brought them into the living room together with a tea tray. "Anton, I've figured out a way to save us some money. I was thinking ... why don't we go on our own instead of a travel agency? You know we have a list with all the hotels on it. All we have to do is make a reservation at one of them. I had in mind one in particular, "The Ollcott" ... the hotel Betty mentioned. I've got it all figured out. We'll take a flight to Montreal and from there we'll take the Amtrak to New York. That way it'll be cheaper. How about it? Once we get there, we'll play it by ear."

Anton yawned. "Yeah, suits me I guess."

"Anton, there's one more thing that's kind of exciting ... we'll get to see Montreal! Too bad we didn't plan this trip sooner. I hate going in November. It might be cold."

She looked at him. He was already dozing, his eyes closed, his head drooping to one side. Some might think his job was easy, but he earned every penny of it. Every day he totally exhausted himself. Long ago she'd learned not to stress him out. But if she left it up to him to decide on a holiday, they'd be staying home.

In mid-week, Anna began packing their bags, noticing how they swelled a little more each day, as she slipped in an extra shawl, her current novel, several pairs of shoes ... one fancy, two sensible for walking. They were leaving in two weeks. She planned to call The Ollcott first thing Monday morning for reservations. The thought that she hadn't done it sooner nagged at her... but there hadn't been time.

Monday morning she picked up Betty's typed list and dialed "The Ollcott" from work, during her coffee break, with full intentions of paying in full for the private call. Honesty was best. One small mistake could cost her her job. She didn't want to work herself into any tight spots.

"The Ollcott. Jerry speaking. How may I help you?"

"Yes, I'd like to make reservations for November 15th, please, for two."

"Sorry, ma'am, but we're booked well into December."

"You're what? Booked did you say?" Disappointment flooded through her. She hung up, knowing that they were still committed to go. She'd already put a deposit on the tickets.

The Amtrak sped past fields that had long been harvested lying in readiness for winter. They whizzed past lakes, small towns, through tunnels and over bridges. Anna drank in the scenery thinking how she would describe it later to Lila and her boys. The decision to go had been hers even though they hadn't been successful in getting a reservation on such short notice. "Don't worry, Anton," she'd said, I'm sure that when we get there we'll find some place to sleep even if it's at the Y. It'll be like an adventure." Now she leaned back into her seat and closed her eyes.

Darkness settled in and she began to worry. Had it been foolish on her part? Too late now. Some time later, she checked the map that the Amtrak had provided, complimentary. "Look Anton, we're almost there." She pointed to a spot along the route.

"Yeah, so I see."

A conductor went by calling out, "Jersey City ... Jersey City."

Passengers around them began to stir. When they'd left Montreal the train had only been half full, now there wasn't a seat to be found.

"This is it, Anton. New York! Get the suitcases off the rack." Excitement and anxiety attacked her at the same time.

Anton reached up into the overhead compartment and her bag came down with a thud. After she'd finished packing both bags were very full.

She tightened the belt on her navy coat and tried to see something out the window. It was pitch dark except for dim shapes illuminated by street lights. The train crawled between gray buildings close enough for her to reach out and touch. A line formed in the aisle. Anna and Anton merged into it.

"Anton, we've stopped."

"Grande Central Station, New York! Folks, the door in the next car is open to your right. Please folks, watch your step as you step down. ... Watch your step, please."

Propelled by the flow, they followed the crowd off the train. Anna stared at a group of teenage boys in black leather with their hair spiked in an outlandish fashion. They went by hooting and whistling.

"Anton, do you realize that this is the famous Grande Central Station? Any phone booths around? Too bad it's already 10:00 o'clock. Look at the domes. I've seen this place on television, you know."

Anton propelled the two bags with difficulty, partly carrying, partly wheeling them along, though they were too unsteady to be wheeled. They stopped before a circular glassed information center. The clerks manning it sat behind microphones, removed and sterile from the general public.

"Shall we ask someone about a hotel?" she asked.

Anton reached into his pocket and adjusted his glasses. "No, let's try the list first."

She felt suddenly nervous, regretting that they hadn't made the reservations before leaving. Who could they ask? There were policemen with dogs throughout the room. Would one of them help?

"Taxi? Taxi?" A black youth in a black and yellow jacket came towards them with a swaying gait. His walk resembled a dance, she thought. He wore a golf cap and stopped directly in front of Anton.

"You folks wanna taxi?"

"Yes, we do," Anna said eagerly, wondering if he could help them. Taxi drivers were knowledgeable about hotels. He might know of one.

"Ya gotta place ta stay?" he asked, as if reading her mind.

"No, but I was about to phone for one," Anton said. "Do you know of a good hotel?"

"Yeah, ah sho do. You folks jus folla me. This yo bags?"

"Yes." Anton put down the receiver and tucked the list back into his pocket.

Anna breathed easier. And they said that cabs in New York were hard to find. It had been easier then she'd imagined.

Anton turned to him. "Do you know where "The Roosevelt" is? I was about to phone "The Roosevelt.""

The youth picked up their bags. "Yeah sah, ah sho do. Ah jus lef a customa deh now. Right diz way. I have ma cab ova hea'."

They stepped out the door. It felt cold and damp, the air heavy laden with the smell of exhaust fumes. He led them to the end of the block, turned right, then started up another block.

"Uh-h-h, where's your cab?" Anna asked, looking around.

"It jus a lil way furer on."

I hope not much further, she thought. Some passersby stopped to stare at them. Now what could be so unusual that they should attract such attention? Was he leading them into an ambush? Anna's stomach took a turn. She forced herself to be calm. Finally, she couldn't contain herself and blurted out once more, "But where's your cab?"

"Not much furer."

"What about the hotel, what's it like? Is it a nice hotel?" she asked, thinking it a good idea to find out something about it.

"Nice? Yeah, sho nice. Ya'all like it. Listen, dey's not much nica, an I wooden be jiven ya."

"But how do you know that they have a room available?"

"Cuz, I jus lef a custama de, das how!"

They followed him across the street and turned left then started up another block.

The boy, puffing by now, put down the weighty suitcases and stopped to catch his breathe. Beads of perspiration covered his face. Anna felt a twinge of guilt remembering all that she'd packed inside.

"Too heavy?" Anton asked. "Listen, why don't you let me carry them a while?"

"No, no! It's awright. Ah'll be okay." He picked up the bags.

Anna noticed that they'd started on a fresh block. She opened her mouth to ask, "How much further?" when dead ahead of her a red neon sign blinked, "The Roosevelt Hotel." She sagged as the tension left in a rush, leaving her limp, weak.

They pushed through a revolving door into warmth and soft light. Her eyes took in the floor. The carpet was a luxurious plush multi-colored red Turkish design. The walls were covered in red and gold wallpaper. Though the hotel had seen better days, it managed to exude an aura of proud elegance. This is perfect, she thought. And it doesn't look too expensive.

The boy put down the suitcases. His eyes darted around the room. Noise and laughter came from the opposite end. He wiped perspiration off his forehead with the back of his arm.

Anna saw a bellhop walk up to a security guard and begin a conversation. The boy became agitated and a look of fear overshadowed his face.

Anton produced his wallet. "Well, sir, what do we owe you?" His hand flipped through the bills.

In a voice barely audible, the boy whispered, "Ah-h-h, nine dollas ... daz $9.95."

"How much?" Anton asked again.

"$9.95," Anna repeated for him, unable to keep the sharpness out of her voice. Would he really charge them that much for walking?

Anton ignored her and turned to the boy once more. "How much did you say?"

The boy, with his eyes on the money came out with, "fifteen dollars. Yeah, fifteen dollars. This time the "fifteen dollars" came out loud and clear.

Anna's anger heightened. Surely Anton wouldn't pay him that much! Unable to contain herself, she burst out. "But he said $9.95 the first time. Didn't you hear him Anton? Think! We walked here. He had no taxi! That's too much for walking!"

Anton's eyes avoided hers. "Here, did you say $15.00? Here's $15.00."

The boy stood dumbfounded before putting the money into his pocket. Anna glared at him. He avoided her gaze. She read guilt and shame written on his face.

A set of stairs faced them leading into the main lobby. Beyond the stairs was a long reception desk. In the middle of the room there was a large circular divan where one could sit and rest.

"Do we carry these bags up to that desk? Anton asked, pointing toward the reception area.

The boy looked up and blinked. "Listen, you done have to carry anythin' anywear." Swiftly he picked up both bags, mounted the stairs and placed them in front of the divan.

Anna felt it was a last ditch attempt on his part to right things between them. She stole a furtive look in his direction.

His head was still down as he muttered, "Thanks," before speeding out of the revolving door.

Anna looked after him with a sense of helplessness. "Why did you do it? Why did you pay him so much? A taxi would have cost us $1.50 at the most. ... Okay, maybe $5.00, but no more."

Anton sighed. "Because I didn't want trouble. And who knows, maybe that's all the money he'll see today. We don't know how he lives. I'm sure he needs it more than we do." He turned away with a sad look on his face.

Anna felt instant contrition. "I see what you mean. But when it was happening, I felt that we were being taken." She suddenly felt ashamed of her outburst, thinking that Anton was a very good man. In fact, he was better than most. Not many would have been willing to pay the boy for walking. Anton did it out of charity.

THE END

THE BEGGAR IN MEXICO

Alisha and Allen Semco walked slowly down a rutted, sun baked street. On both sides Alisha noticed houses run down, dilapidated and crumbling. The sun beat down intensely hot. She felt her dress fastened to her back by the sweat pouring from her body. Her left arm, covered by a fiberglass cast, felt prickly and uncomfortable. She and Allen had chosen Mexico for a holiday many times, but this was the first time they'd picked Acapulco.

Their home was in Edmonton, Alberta, where Allen worked in the judicial system as a judge. Now with the three children, a boy and two girls all married, it was an ideal time to travel. They liked to vacation in some steamy, exotic place to get away from the cold winters in Western Canada. Allen also had a five week vacation which encouraged the trips abroad.

Only four days ago they had flown in by chartered jet to occupy one of the newest hotels in Acapulco Bay, "The Copacabana." It was obvious that it was still under construction because the patio had no guard rail around it. Alisha thought it rather dangerous, especially since their room was on the thirteenth floor. The view overlooked a glittering sea. Alisha, who was born on the prairies, liked the sound of the waves crashing on the shoreline. It was the first sound she heard upon waking up and the last sound before drifting off to sleep. It's monotony imprinted a hypnotic lulling effect upon her senses.

At the moment, the relentless heat of the day was providing little comfort. She took in the deteriorating houses close to the sidewalk with a worried look.

"Allen, take note this isn't the best part of town. We could easily be robbed, you know." Fear raised her voice a trifle higher than usual, as she tried in vain to alert her husband to the possibilities of unforeseen danger.

"Don't worry, it's quite safe. I'll protect you," he assured her, sarcastically.

Alisha sighed, and trudged on without another word. There was little that he was afraid off and in view of her own anxieties, she wished fervently that she had some of his confidence, his self assurance. A more relaxed attitude would most assuredly contribute to a happier life, she thought.

It was high noon and they were on their way to the people's market. They'd taken a taxi to the first market, attractively set up for tourists. Alisha had shopped through colorful dresses, gold rings, long dangling earrings and every kind of leather purse imaginable, keeping in mind to bring back something for each of the family at home. However

Allen, who soon tired of looking at the same stock wherever they went, had suggested something different.

"You know, I noticed a sign across from our hotel that said there's a Government market just 400 meters away from here. How would you like to go see it?"

"Yes, why not. All these touristy places do look the same, don't they? So why not?"

Now as they walked, she was overwhelmed by the poverty so evident all around them and was having second thoughts. No matter which way she looked it was not a pleasant scene. At their hotel they were protected from such sights. From time to time a stench assailed her, drifting in from open sewers and raw garbage festering in the streets. Dark skinned children played in the open air, calling to each other as they raced by.

"Allen, I don't see any other tourists here but us, are you sure it's safe?" she asked, frowning and anxious. "You know we might be a target. I'm carrying money, all kinds of travelers cheques ... you've got a camera. Look around, everybody else is Mexican, we're the only odd couple."

He didn't say a word, but threw her an annoyed look. They plodded on. It was the siesta hour and the hottest part of the day when most Mexicans were indoors resting. They weren't as foolish as the tourists who were everywhere at all hours of the day or night.

Alisha scanned the view ahead searching for other sightseers. The road they were walking on had narrowed and an arrow with a sign below pointed the way to the market.

A taxi drove by carrying a carload of tourists. Alisha's fears leveled off, certain now that they were going in the right direction.

She yearned for shade. It was at least 100 degrees and very humid. Might be nice to sit down ... anything to escape the heat. Now more shops fanned out before them. They were approaching what looked like a large warehouse. Both front and back entrances were open allowing a breeze to flow through. They walked in to escape the scorching rays of the sun, their faces glistening with perspiration.

Two weeks before they'd left, Alisha had had the misfortune to break her arm while walking over a snow covered, icy driveway. In view of the extreme heat, she tried to imagine the cold that they'd left behind and couldn't begin to fathom it.

She longed for something to drink. At the opposite end of the building stood a counter with pop in crates piled beside it. The cement floor was littered with dust and empty pop bottles. Square metal folding tables stood at random here and there. There were several tourists drinking cola and talking to each other at some of the tables.

Allen paused and turned to her. "Would you like a Coke?"

"Yes, yes, I would," she answered, much relieved that her worries had been unfounded, that they were safe and that they could sit down to rest and refresh themselves. Behind the counter a young Mexican girl looked up to take Allen's order.

"Two Cokes please."

She pulled two bottles out of a crate beside her, opened them and handed him the drinks. "Eighty pesos, senor."

Alisha took all the change from the bottom of her purse and gave it to Allen. He counted out the correct amount before giving it to the clerk. The remainder he dropped into his pocket. With the Mexican peso dropping in value, Alisha was obliged to keep the money in her handbag because it was too awkward to carry the big coins in a wallet.

They sat down at one of the folding tables. Alisha took a sip of her Coke and leaned back. At that very moment, a Mexican woman dressed in a black dress and a black shawl wrapped over her shoulders, came gliding into the room. A strange smile played on the woman's face. She looked around the warehouse, took note of everyone, then approached one of the tables holding out her hand. Must be a beggar, Alisha thought.

Suddenly, she was beside their table. Alisha's first instinct was to put something into her outstretched palm. Too late she remembered giving all the pesos to Allen. However, begging is discouraged in Mexico and tourists are informed by their guides not to give anything to the many beggars in the streets. She knew that Allen, who was law conscious, would certainly object as well.

But she turned to him and whispered, "Give her something."

She looked up to see that he was already shaking his head. With seeming unconcern, the woman walked to the next table where a man in a straw hat and his wife sat drinking ginger ale, his fair skin flushed red from the heat.

The woman held out her hand at their table. But the tourist, without so much as a glance in her direction, merely shook his head.

She turned, still with the same strange smile on her face. She was about to try another table when her eyes caught sight of Alisha's broken arm in the cast. She whirled about and returned to where they sat.

This time a rapid flow of words in Spanish came out of her mouth, as she tried in vain to communicate with Alisha and Allen. Slowly she withdrew her left arm from the folds of her shawl.

Alisha gasped in surprise. It looked just the same as her wrist had looked when she'd broken it before the doctor had had a chance to set it. In this position, the woman's hand would be totally useless. Alisha could see the break where the bones protruded in a V at the wrist. It would make movement stiff and painful, in fact... impossible.

Alisha listened to her, trying in vain to make sense of her words as she kept talking. She kept repeating 'tres ans' which Alisha took to mean that she had been in this state for three years. The woman kept up the one sided conversation with Alisha straining to understand. Within her, the woman had aroused a deep compassion for her dilemma. Now she deeply regretted not having kept even one peso in her purse. Her eyes flooded with tears. Keeping her head down, she whispered, "Allen, please give her something ... my arm looked exactly like that before it was set."

Without a word, Allen reached into his pocket and produced a handful of Mexican coins which he handed to her.

The flow of words stopped. She smiled and made a sign of the cross over Alisha's arm. Then she blessed her and said a prayer. Slowly she turned and walked away from them, carrying the pesos.

Alisha noticed that a shrine had been set up at one end of the room. A large wooden cross stood on a raised platform with wreaths and vases of flowers surrounding it. In front of the cross stood a twelve inch picture of the Virgin Mary holding Jesus. The woman walked to the shrine and knelt in front of it. There was a jar on the platform which was used as a receptacle for contributions. She bowed her head in worship.

Alisha turned back to Allen and was about to say something when she heard the clink of money falling into the jar. She turned her head in time to see the woman rise and glide silently out of the building. She was smiling. She looked unconcerned and happy.

"Allen, did you see that? Did you see what she did with the money you gave her?" she asked in amazement.

"Yes, she put it into that jar for the church."

"I wonder why her wrist was never set?"

"Who knows!"

"Well, what did you think of her?"

He pondered a moment. "You know, I'd say there was an ethereal quality about her. Strange ... that look she had on her face...it was as if she didn't have a care in the world, almost as if she wasn't of this world."

Later Alisha thought about the beggar woman. Why would she give up her last peso when she seemed in such desperate need herself? And why had nothing been done to set her wrist straight? Was this a reflection of man's compassion? Was there no charity left in anyone? Especially when the beggar woman had so much charity herself.

Questions crowded through her mind unanswered. Certainly her arm could have been straightened out even by the most primitive of methods. It would only take someone to pull it straight and tie it between two splints. Why was it neglected? What about her family? Did no one care about her?

Although Alisha and Allen returned to the market they did not see her again. Their lives had touched but briefly. She'd made a lasting impression upon Alisha who wondered whether she had said a prayer for their salvation before that altar. Judging from the smile on her face it was quite evident that she had found hers.

After they returned home, the cast was removed from Alisha's arm. The break had healed perfectly and she wondered if the prayers of the beggar woman had helped with the healing?

THE END

THE ADVICE

It was Sunday and Tanya sat next to Walter, her husband, in a pew at St. Edmunds Catholic church. They were both in their senior years, retired, with Tanya still taking an active part in the church choir. However, today she was thankful that it wasn't her turn to lead the congregation. Emily Stark was in charge of the singing. She had a most beautiful voice, cultured, clear as a bell, sounded trained. It was a sublime pleasure to listen to her.

On the Sundays that she didn't have to sing, Tanya always paid special attention to the prayers and worship. Her flowered dress revealed a slight form, about five feet two and attractive. Her hair was cut short. It framed a heart shaped face with brown eyes and full lips.

Norman Price sat two pews over and directly in front of her and Walter. Now every time Tanya looked at Norman, she was filled with dread. She wondered what she should do? Would she tell him today? Should she tell him? Did she have the right? The nerve? She glanced at Walter, sitting next to her. Tall, thin, still handsome, his jawline firm, his eyes on the priest, no inkling of what was going on in her head. He looked unapproachable. I won't tell him, she thought. It would create such trouble. How could she make him see or understand her purpose?

Norman, all 350 lbs. of him, sat half reclining, his legs spread out in front, his hands over his belly with the fingers touching, as though protecting that belly. He was a mountain of flesh.

Rachael, his wife, had come early, even before the service began. They sat apart as they usually did every Sunday. Rachael, several pews over, looked charming, her blond hair in a downward sweep, parted at an angle just wide enough to reveal a vivacious smile, perfect teeth and sparkling blue eyes.

Norman had come late and had slipped in when the service was nearly half over.

That morning the minute that she saw Rachael, Tanya had stopped her to ask, "Where's Norman?"

Rachael, somewhat surprised at the question, had replied, "He's sick. He went to the doctor and the doctor upped his blood pressure pills. Last night he had chest pains again. He was up about 1:00 or 2:00 in the morning. I was worried. The doctor gave him something for angina. He's diabetic, you know."

Upon hearing this news, Tanya was beside herself. Now more certain than ever that somehow she was to play a part in his life.

She tried to concentrate on the music, on the priest, then the organist and even Walter. It was no use. Again, she felt her insides on fire. Every nerve taut, red hot. Her eyes kept straying to Norman and the question burning in her mind. She started a prayer for him. She'd been on the same prayer since Monday, wondering if that was to be her mission?

Now she cried out within herself, "Lord Jesus! Lord Jesus! Just how am I supposed to help him?"

A week ago on Monday, a fine day in June, she was working in her spotless kitchen, singing a hymn with her mind on God and the church, when out of the clear blue she'd had a distinct vision of Norman. She could see him pacing in a field of green grass. Walking back and forth, back and forth.

On Tuesday the same vision came flooding back with Norman walking back and forth in green grass.

When it was repeated on Wednesday, the questions began. What was the Lord trying to tell her? It must be the Lord, she thought. Who else could it be? But Lord, what is my job? Am I to say to him that it's dangerous for him to be so fat? How will he react? I'm sure many people, including his wife, have told him that.

At times she got distracted and the vision wasn't there. But it returned every time she thought of him. And it would not go away!

Again she felt her insides burning. She leaned back in the pew and tried in vain to relax, all the time knowing that she would do as the Lord instructed. The thought made her intensely nervous thinking of Norman and how he'd react to "the advice." A person's weight was such a personal, private thing.

For Tanya, the mass went by in a blur. As soon as it finished, she went to the front to get the wafers to distribute for Holy Communion. The moment she dreaded was approaching. It made her nervous just thinking that he'd be very angry with her. She imagined him coming down hard on her. She imagined that he'd tell others in the church what a horrible person she was telling him such a thing. She felt unforgivably sinful.

She finished passing out the wafers. Her eyes rested on Norman. She noticed that there were some people beside him smiling and talking to him. Isn't there anyone else in this church that is concerned enough about his weight to help him? Why doesn't someone tell him the truth? she wondered, angrily. The church started to empty quickly.

Now ... I'll tell him now, she thought. She walked to where he stood and touched his arm. Oh my God, what am I doing?

"Norman, I have to talk to you. By ourselves, please."

He moved toward her and away from those standing close to him.

"Norman, you need to lose weight!"

He drew back, shocked. Anger took over. She could tell he wasn't about to accept it.

"Norman, have you ever thought about eating differently?"

"Nope! And I'm sick to death about people telling me. I'm fed up with people meddling. Right up to here." His hand went in a sweeping motion halfway up his face to indicate just how "fed up" he really was. He moved away from her.

She followed after him. "Norman wait! I have the greatest compassion for you. And I have great soul for you. I feel a lot of sorrow for you, too! You can think of me as an intermediary. I thought I'd tell you that. My husband, Walter, he had a heart attack four years ago. We had to completely change our life. We had to eat differently. It wasn't easy!"

He looked at her with distaste. "I hadn't thought about it. And I'm not going to do anything about it."

Tanya wasn't finished with him yet. "Norman, what happened last Monday or Tuesday?"

"Nothing."

"Think back. What happened?"

"Oh, I went to see the doctor."

"I had this vision of you on Monday, on Tuesday, and I think Wednesday as well. I could see you walking around in ...in green grass. For some reason I got the impression that you were going to lose weight that way ... walking back and forth. Well, walking anyway."

Norman looked defiant. The dread of what she'd just said settled in her gut. What have I done? she wondered. Walter doesn't even know! How could I do this? But she pressed on, as though driven.

"Don't you think you're in complete denial when you say you're never going to change your eating habits? ... That's total denial, Norman."

His lips pressed together. "I don't care."

Tanya felt outright disgust for herself. Enough, she thought. I've done enough. Within herself, she felt like a real sinner. She turned and flitted down the aisle to get away from him. Father Gabriel was coming towards them. He was approaching quickly. Had he noticed the look on Norman's face ... or hers when they were talking? As she flew past him she called out, "Hi, Father!" Then she slid out of the church as quickly as possible.

Walter was waiting for her by the door. Now I'll have to tell him, she thought.

She related the scene that had just taken place between her and Norman to Walter ... but not entirely everything, leaving out the part about Norman being angry. She toned it down, praying that he'd understand and not chastise her too severely.

He looked at her in disbelief. "Tanya, you'll have to learn to control your tongue! That's all there's to it."

They got into the truck. "Walter, the intent in my heart was good."

"Yeah, I know it was."

"Walter, what should I do? Should I apologize to him?"

"No, no, leave him alone. Don't say anything. You've done enough damage."

"You mean I can't even say "good morning" to him anymore?"

"You could say "good morning" but nothing else. Don't say anything else!"

The week began. It was a horrible week. She couldn't stop thinking about it. She felt as if she'd taken an axe and hit Norman on the head with it. She prayed and rehearsed everything she would say to him. And each time she'd shoot the thought down and find something different to replace it with.

She pictured herself coming to him and saying... "I don't know what came over me. I don't know what I was thinking. I'm such a sinner! Can you forgive me?" Then she'd think of something different because nothing was ever good enough. And so it kept rolling around in her head.

At night, she slept out of pure necessity. Most of the time awake, she tossed endlessly. Her "problem" and what she had done was always waiting for her. She could not rid herself of it.

She met her two sisters, Alisha and Anna, for a buffet lunch on the following Thursday. It was Anna's birthday. On birthdays they always got together to celebrate. Tanya's mind was not on food, so the lunch was spoiled for her.

As soon as Walter got up to get some coffee, as soon as he was totally out of earshot, she whispered her dilemma to them. "What should I do?" she asked. "I feel so bad, we may have to change churches. I've already considered it. Except that I can't find another church that I'd like to go to. Do you think I should apologize?"

Anna observed her in shock. "Don't say another word! Just shut up!" Anton, her husband, agreed with her.

Alisha turned to her. "Yeah, just leave it alone."

"You know, I really like Rachael his wife. She's such a nice lady. I hate to give her up. She always gives me such nice hugs and I hug her back. She's so sweet! A pretty lady! Intelligent! I mean she's pretty on the inside and out. And she prays." She left the restaurant without resolving anything.

With dread Tanya waited for Sunday to come. At the same time not really wanting it to come when she imagined what was waiting for her from Norman. She didn't even know his last name. He was just someone she happened to know at the church. She'd asked Rachael for her phone number. Though Tanya heard her say it, she couldn't remember it. She even considered buying a card with an apology already written in it.

On Sunday, her heart pounding, she went to church. She had decided that she would somehow, whether he accepted it or not, get an apology over to Norman.

As they walked into the church, they met Rachael standing in the foyer. She was smiling.

Tanya sidled up to her with lowered her head. "Rachael, I am so sorry!"

Tanya raised her head. Rachael was still smiling.

"Tanya, it helped! It helped! After your talk with Norman, we went shopping for groceries. We bought all kinds of green lettuce and vegetables to eat."

"But Rachael, how will he ever forgive me for what I said? I felt so awful after. I spent the week in misery just thinking about it."

"Tanya, he's fine. He's forgiven you."

"I'm not so sure, Rachael."

They went in. Norman was in his usual place. What Rachael said was encouraging, but she couldn't quite accept it. It was her turn to sing. She had to go past Norman to get to the front where the organ was. She broke into a sweat knowing this. Now very perturbed, she removed her white jacket, thinking that she didn't want her perspiration staining it.

She remembered Walter telling her to leave Norman alone and not to say anymore to him than "good morning." She put a genuine smile on her face, or at least what she thought was a genuine smile, and forged ahead. She touched his hand as she went by, "Good morning, Norman."

To her utter surprise he grabbed her hand and exclaimed, "I want to speak to you after mass!"

She nodded. "Yes, of course." She kept going to the front.

Even at this point she didn't know what it meant; she felt it could go either way. During the mass a thread of hope that all was forgiven kept circling in her mind. She kept seeing Rachael's smiling face. However, Rachael might think it was all right, but not necessarily Norman.

The mass was over. She felt very anxious. Her legs trembling, Tanya couldn't wait any longer and went straightway to where Norman stood waiting for her.

"Did you say you wanted to speak with me?"

"Yes!" ... For a moment, he just looked at her before he burst out, "Who would have thought that Mighty Mouse would come out with boxing gloves on and would hit me right here," he touched his nose, "with a two by four." Norman laughed a hearty laugh.

All the tension rushed out of her. "Oh, Norman! I had a terrible week. I was rehearsing all the speeches I was going to say to you."

"And I was rehearsing all week what I was going to say to you. And it wasn't good. I was so angry with you, I had to confess it to the priest. Yes, angry, I was! ... But you know what? I really needed that wakeup call! Bless you! Bless you! Bless you!" Suddenly he grabbed her, he hugged her and kissed her on the cheek.

Tanya, overwhelmed, kissed him back. Then she flew to tell Walter what had happened between her and Norman.

THE END

THE THIEF

Paul Briggs surveyed the house from a safe distance before deciding to come closer. He could bet his black leather jacket that there wasn't anyone home. The house was built low, California style, well kept lawn ... probably lawn service ... dark brown cedar siding and slant roof with shakes. Expensive! Thirty minutes ago the old lady had taken off in a Cadillac to go shopping. He knew the people by name. Edwards. The guy was a lawyer. Everybody in Whitecourt knew him.

It looked easy. He went to the back lane to check out an escape route ... just in case. The key word was speed. To get inside, steal whatever was worth stealing and leave as fast as possible. It could be done really quick. Ricky Hanson would never believe that he did it, especially in broad daylight. Who would suspect such brazenness? He peered through a crack in the vertical six foot cedar fence and noticed a small ladder lying beside the garden. He lifted the latch and slipped inside.

Paul took a quick look around the house, careful to avoid the front. It paid to be careful. At the far end away from the street, he found what he was looking for ... a partially open window. Since it was in the back part of the house, he figured it must be a bedroom window.

He raised his arm. The sill was just inches short of his fingers. He stopped and ran to get the ladder. It didn't go as high as he would have liked, but it would do. He smiled, thinking what fools they were to leave it there. He popped out the screen easily enough and dropped it to the ground, then raised up the window. A beige sheer curtain hid the view and tangled with his fingers.

Next door a dog began to bark in a frenzy. How annoying! He half glanced over his shoulder at the excited yapping from a small, black curly haired pup, snarling and biting at a spot in the fence that separated them. So bark, he thought.

He hadn't noticed anything moving in the house next door. He took another step up the ladder, then put both hands on the inside of the room. He'd have to use muscle if he was going to make it. With patient persistence he began a slow wriggle upwards, positioning himself to fall in head first.

At first it was so faint, so remote that he didn't pay attention to the sound, but when it persisted and grew louder, he gave pause hoping it wasn't what the rational part of his brain was warning him about.

Had someone turned him in? But who? There was no one around that could have seen him ... he'd checked. He held his breathe in hope. The sound came closer. Suddenly hope died when he heard the screeching of brakes come to a grinding stop in front of the house.

Panic seized him and he pushed harder. If he could get inside he might be able to hide. With inches to go and only a small portion of his legs showing there was still a chance. He began to perspire. Now unable to stop, he kept working his way in.

"Okay son, that's far enough." Strong fingers gripped his ankles and wouldn't let go.

A sickening crunch traveled through his stomach, as invisible hands began to reverse his action, tugging him back until he stood with both feet on the ground.

The policeman was tall, well built, with a German Shepherd at his side. The dog bared his teeth and growled at him.

"Down boy."

Paul looked up to see a stream of uniformed cops coming up the walk. "Dammit! Shit!"

He made a snap decision. He ducked, then twisting out of the policeman's grasp, he bolted toward the fence, remembering that he could outrun any kid in school.

"Don't let the kid get away! ... Grab him, Harry!"

It was absurd for him to try to get away, but he had to try. From behind he heard giant footsteps pounding after him. With one mighty effort he sprang for the boards. Someone grabbed him by the jeans. A blow landed to the side of his head. It stunned him as he struggled to free himself before a gray mist swept over his eyes. He fell back. The mist cleared. He gasped out, "I thought you sons of bitches weren't supposed to do that!"

"Watch your mouth kid. Read him his rights, Harry."

"What rights? He can't be more'n thirteen. Well, look at him! I'd be wasting my time."

"Okay, okay, kid, up ya go. You're coming with me. I'm Constable Shubert. Now be nice'n friendly and tell me your name." He pinched on a pair of handcuffs then pointed him toward the police car.

A sullen silence followed the question. What would Ricky say when he didn't come home? Dejection swept over him. If it wasn't for the pig cops, he'd be halfway across town by now.

"Uh-h-h, Paul Briggs, I guess."

The policeman looked incredulous. "Paul Briggs? Are you the kid that Sergeant Nichols picked up last week for the same thing?"

He dropped his head. "I ain't sayin."

"Kid, how old are you?"

"Fourteen. So what? So what're you gonna do with me? Huh? You gonna tell my Mommy?"

"I'm putting you into a holding cell for one thing and you're going to be charged for another. How's that for starters? So don't get too smartass with me."

"A holding cell? What for? You can't keep me in no cell!"

"Yes, we can. That's the law, kid. We'll keep you until Judge Semco comes in. Let's see." He flipped through a book. "You're in luck, he comes Thursday. That's three days from now. You won't be able to get out any sooner because someone has to bail you out. And it's the judge that sets the bail."

His face paled. His slight form slumped. He didn't think that either Mrs. Hanson or her old man would worry enough to bail him out. In fact, they'd be damn happy that he was in jail because he'd be separated from their precious Ricky.

"You got a family, kid?"

"No, I ain't got a family." He mimicked.

"You a run away?" The constable looked serious. "Where do you live? You gotta tell me, because I aim to find out ... sooner or later."

"And what if I am! What's it to you? You ain't sending me back no where, because I ain't going."

"Okay, have it your way."

They stopped at the Police Station and went inside.

"I gotta make out a report. Look, just tell me where you hang out." He steered him toward the back to the special cell reserved for juveniles.

"I gotta search you, kid. And I want the shoe laces from your runners."

"What for?"

"Just a precaution. We don't want you trying anything funny."

The Constable made the search.

"What have we here. Switch blades are illegal, or didn't you know?" He opened the cell door.

"So what?" Paul stopped. "I ain't going in there! You can't make me." He took a step backwards.

"Sorry, kid. Get inside." The Constable shoved him in and the door clanged shut.

Stupid! Dumb! Stupid! He thought with disgust at himself. The pigs got him. He kicked at the bars. The sound echoed through the corridor. But what could he expect? He was an amateur. Maybe it was better then being at Ricks' and having to listen to Mrs. Hanson go on and on pointing out that he should be looking for a place of his own. Well this drab cell was a place of his own. A grey blanket covered a cot in a corner. The window had gray bars. A sink, a toilet, gray concrete floor. He sank down on the cot.

At six a guard came in with his supper. Meatloaf, mashed potatoes, carrots and a roll. There were stewed peaches for dessert. He forced himself to swallow some of the food, but it was hard going down. At nine, when the lights went out, he lay down and tried to sleep.

The face of Nancy Arnholt sprang into view. Tall, thin, with blonde stringy hair. Her eyes, recessed into a vague world of dreams, were but a blank stare. He saw himself and others like himself waving to her, as Seth her old man helped her into a truck. She stared at them through the window. A tear trickled down her cheek.

That was the last they'd seen of her. She was the closest thing to caring for him that he'd ever experienced. He sensed her concern for all of them. But it hadn't lasted. She hadn't been able to cope with her inner trials.

Including himself, Nancy had looked after seven foster children. Right after her breakdown, old man Arnholt started drinking. Nights, he quaffed down drink after drink until he passed out. Usually the boys stumbled upon him in the morning lying in a disgusting mess of vomit and pee. He'd had enough sense to hold on to the children because they were his only source of income when his construction business went down hill. Now every time Olivia Benson, the social worker, came to the house he spruced himself up, whipping everyone into action to get the place tidied up. Generally, it stank of unwashed dishes and urine, with pots of food lining the kitchen counter and stove.

One never knew what the closely packed refrigerator held, bursting with its many jars and bottles. Some had green mold encrusted at the top, giving off a rank odor whenever the door was opened. Mrs. Arnholt, after she became sick, had stopped cleaning it.

There were clothes stacked up in piles on chairs and on beds. He'd learned to sleep over or under them, often dumping everything on the floor in angry frustration, while searching for a blanket.

None of the boys had families that cared for them. His own mother, Sarah Briggs, had given him up for adoption. No wonder she didn't care what happened to him. She was a drunk. There were no eager parents waiting to adopt him.

Old man Arnholt let it slip about his mother being a drunk by mistake one time when Paul questioned him. His birth certificate stated "unknown" where the father's name went. A knot tightened in his stomach every time he thought of her.

Running away had always been in the back of his mind. That, and finding her ... his mother.

He'd made the decision when his stay at Arnholt's had taken a turn for the worse. Especially after Louie and Stewart Blaine had beat him up for taking a pair of Louie's jeans because his were in shreds. He was no match for big Stewart, Louie's older brother. However, he had to admire them. They stuck together like glue, with Stewart overshadowing Louie like some sissy grandmother. "Next time it happens, I'll kill you." Stewart had warned him, brandishing a big stiletto.

That night he went into Louie's room, stole Louie's jeans, his stiletto, and left Arnholt's.

Later on he ran into Ricky Hanson on the street. Paul remembered from school that he'd been a soft touch. Why not ask him for a place to stay?

"Rick, uh-h-h, just for a couple of days till I can find my own place and get a job." As of today, it was already two weeks and no job.

He turned over and pulled the rough blanket over his head shutting his eyes tight. If he didn't let go, he'd explode. He pictured the guard finding him in a million pieces in the morning. He groaned and allowed the tears to flow over his face not willing to admit even to himself that he had feelings. After a time he fell asleep to relive the scene of his capture.

Judge Allen Semco smoothed the royal blue lapels of his black Provincial Judge's gown, and straightened a small white tie under his chin. The robe and vestments added an air of dignity to the Court.

He glanced at himself in the mirror over the sink of his private bathroom. He was of average height with intense, deep set brown eyes and a rigid jaw line. He was proud of his record to accurately asses the many cases that he dealt with.

To figure out who was lying and who was telling the truth wasn't always easy, but he had a knack. Not many of his cases were overturned in appeal court. He was a "no nonsense" type of judge. His motto was 'cut the crap and just give me the facts.'

He picked up the afternoon docket. There was one case set for the afternoon. A knock sounded. Miss Hudson, the court clerk, pushed aside the door and called out. "We're waiting, sir."

"Be right there." He smoothed back his graying hair and entered the courtroom to hear the clerk calling the room to order. "All rise in the name of Her Majesty the Queen. Judge Allen Semco presiding. Please be seated."

He scanned the police report, then the prisoner at the podium.

Paul's curly black hair was swept back, giving his face a dead white look.

Allen Semco read the report first checking the boy's age. "This court is now in session." He turned to the prisoner. "Paul Briggs, the charge against you states that on July 18th, 1974, you were caught breaking and entering into the home of Mr. and Mrs. Edwards. It states here that you were caught on the same charge two other times before this ... and were let off by a reprimand both times. Is that correct?"

"Yes, sir."

"You were also caught shoplifting a portable radio. A charge that Mr. Maines from the Handy Hardware refused to press charges on, even though he called the police. I believe he said it was because of your age."

"Yes, sir."

Judge Allen Semco looked at the boy with a twinge of concern. With his slight build, he looked no more then thirteen. Still a child by all appearances. He sighed. "Paul, it states here that you ran away from your foster home. This will be the third time. I might add that you stole some jeans and a knife from another boy about your age at Mr. Seth Arnholts' residence. Is this correct?"

His mouth drooped. A sadness came over his face. "Yes, sir."

"How do you wish to plead? Do you understand these charges against you?"

"Guilty sir. I wish to plead guilty."

"But do you understand the charges?"

"Yes sir, I think so. Constable Shubert he explained them to me." His pupils, enlarged with fear, projected the iris a darker blue then ordinary.

"Paul, I don't know whether you realize this, but these are all serious charges. All indictable offenses. And your actions indicate a flaunting of the law, a disrespect for conformity. Have you anything to say in your defense?"

He hung his head. "No, sir."

"Paul Briggs, it is the duty of the court to sentence you to three months at the Bowden Correctional Institute for Young Offenders. After which time you will be placed on probation for another six months."

Paul felt himself weaken. He was going to jail. He hadn't counted on a sentence. "But sir?"

"Yes?"

"Nothing." He shook his head. There was no one in the courtroom that he recognized. Ricky Hanson hadn't shown up even though he'd telephoned him the second day. On the phone he'd promised that he would. He'd have to go it alone.

"Case dismissed." Judge Semco turned to the policeman in charge. "Constable Shubert, I'll see the boy in my chambers ... alone."

Judge Semco leaned against the desk and faced Paul. Their eyes met. The boy did his best to be casual and take it "like a man."

"I had them bring you here because I want to say something to you. Paul, you're starting your life all wrong. You're young. Do you want to be a criminal?"

"No, sir."

"In the future you've got to get it into your mind to go straight. You're getting in deeper and deeper. I'd hate to see you wreck your life. It would be such a waste. One mistake leads to another. Under the circumstances, I gave you the lightest sentence I could. I'm guided by the law, too. Nobody is exempt. First thing, when you're in Bowden, because you're only fourteen, you'll have to attend school. Paul, I'm telling you this for your own good. Put some effort into it. Schooling will get you a good job. If you try, you can still make something of yourself. It's not too late. But it'll be up to you. You can't keep repeating this ...this pattern that you seem to have set for yourself."

Paul's head dropped. At his feet two spots appeared where his tears fell. Judge Semco heard a muffled cry. Suddenly he felt thin bony arms encircle his waist. Man and boy stood together in an emotional grip.

"It's alright, child, don't cry. There, there, don't cry. Just do as I say. Study hard. Do your best, always your best. This will all pass. You'll be fine. I just know it."

The boy's frame convulsed with sobs. Allen Semco brought out a monogrammed hanky and wiped his own eyes, then the boy's.

He thought of his own son, "Dan." He looked a lot like this boy. Dark haired, pale faced, but built stronger, taller. Dan had good upstanding morals, good discipline, great study habits. The boy could learn from him. They'd be good company for each other.

His home could provide the stability that he needed so desperately. But what about Alisha, his wife? How would she view his bringing home a runaway? A knock sounded on the door. "Sir?"

Instinctively the boy let go. He stopped crying and dried his eyes with the back of his hand, as Constable Shubert entered the room.

The Judge turned to him. "Goodbye Paul." He shook his hand. "Remember what I told you. Promise me you'll try? Will you do it for me?"

"Yes, sir. I'll try, sir."

The Constable guided Paul out the door. Paul turned to look back at the judge. A warm feeling spread throughout his gut. He could do it. He knew he could. For someone like this judge, he could go straight. He had to have something to hold on to, even if it was only the advice of a judge who'd just sentenced him.

After they left, Judge Allen Semco sat staring at the spot where the boy had stood, where the boy had cried. He longed to help him, and for one wild moment he had been tempted to offer his home as a sanctuary to the boy. But he'd let it pass, prompted by a code of ethics never to get involved with the cases, at the same time wishing that he had the guts to break that code. He picked up his briefcase, removed his gown and left for home, with the boy still pulling at his heart and his mind.

Time and again, the boy made an entry into the Judge's thoughts. He wasn't easy to forget. On impulse, he decided to keep track of Paul and instructed Constable Shubert to keep him informed of what was happening at the Bowden Correctional Institute.

A year later, the Constable stopped by to talk to the judge about Paul.

"He's done his time Sir, and he's been released. He's living with a family that had taken him in while he was on parole. A good family, I hear. They say he wants to finish High School. One more thing, he likes cars, so he plans to be a mechanic."

A genuine smile spread over the judge's face. "Constable Shubert, that's very good news. Glad to hear it."

"Sir, I believe that you helped him. In fact that's what he's telling everybody who'll listen, that a judge helped him."

That day Judge Allen Semco left the Whitecourt Courthouse satisfied that he'd made a change in Paul's life, a change for the better. It brought a lump to his throat thinking that the boy had actually taken his advice.

Judge Semco turned the wheel of his Eldorado Cadillac into the Fixit Right Garage. The car needed an oil change and one tire seemed to be losing air. He got out of the car intent on catching the attention of the mechanic on duty.

"Excuse me. I'd like an oil change and could someone check the tires ..." He stopped. The face in front of him looked familiar. It had been three years. The boy was now a man. He found himself looking into Paul's eyes. He broke into a smile. "Paul! Good to see you! How are you? Are you working here?"

Paul smiling, held out his hand to him. "Yes, sir. One more year and I'll be a licensed mechanic. Thanks to you I'm doing great sir. Just great!"

"Paul, I can't take all the credit for that. It was your hard work that did it. Paul, I'm proud of you, really proud. You've come a long way."

"Thank you, sir. I just kept remembering what you said to me that day in your courtroom. It kept me going. Sir, I'll personally look after your car."

"Thanks, Paul. I'm sure you will." Judge Semco turned away with a warm feeling inside him.

THE END

FOR THE LOVE OF A STRANGER

Tanya breathed deeply, as she walked briskly to work that Monday morning. Though she was pressed for time, she had no intentions of being late. It was already 7:50 and work at the Federal Building began at 8:00.

It was early spring and the air was filled with the sweet fragrance of leaves and grass about to come through the layer of dust which had settled on dried grass since fall. If she wasn't so rushed she could certainly have enjoyed it more. The snow was mostly melted. The sky was a cobalt blue and a cool wind caressed her at times, blowing her blonde hair over her face.

Though still early, she noticed a lot of people along Jasper Avenue, the down town main street of Edmonton, Alberta, a city where she and Walter Kushinsky, her husband, lived. She thought about dinner and wondered what she would serve for the two of them. Walter had a hearty appetite and she usually prepared a lot of food to satisfy his cravings. Though looking at him you wouldn't know it because he was as thin as a rail.

Tanya stepped aside, as a group of office workers hurried past her. She glanced at her watch wondering now if five minutes would really be enough time to make it to work?

Her eyes turned back to the sidewalk. Suddenly she stopped and stood stock still. Directly in front of her, at her very feet, she saw a homeless man, an elderly man lying as though passed out. Another swarm of people went by. They actually had to get off the sidewalk to avoid stepping on him. He was shabbily dressed and looked to be in his eighties.

Tanya bent over him determined to check if he was alive. She touched his shoulder . "Sir, excuse me. Sir, good morning!"

His eyes flickered when she spoke. He looked as if he might be waking up.

"Can I help you get up?"

He moved again. Tanya took his arm and helped him to a sitting position. She noticed that by now the sidewalk was even more crowded than before. It was odd that the people who passed them would not make eye contact with her or the stranger. Both could have been invisible. No one stopped to ask what he was doing sitting in the middle of the sidewalk.

"Can you stand up?"

"Yes," he answered while still sitting. He gave her a strange look."You know, last night I was at the Mayfair Bar an' I got drunk. I dunno what happened, but when I came to, somebody took my wallet. I don't have a nickel on me."

"Well lets get you up. Come now!"

Tanya coaxed him up till he was on his feet. She noticed that he was unsteady and trembling.

"Let me buy you breakfast."

He shook his head.

She looked to see where they could go for breakfast. There was a restaurant across the street from where they stood, but in his present condition, I'd have to physically drag him, she thought. It's such a busy intersection, he couldn't possibly cross that street. And with all that traffic, it would be impossible. However, only a block away and on the same side that they were on, she remembered passing a small coffee shop.

"Come on, let's go." Now determined to get him there, she took his arm and got him walking in the direction of the restaurant. She opened the door and they went in. There was an empty booth directly in front of them. He sat down with a thud.

"Now, how about some bacon, eggs, toast, coffee..."

He interrupted her before she finished. "No! No! I can't eat. No breakfast, please, please! I've been drinking. If I eat, I'll throw up!"

"Then how about some coffee?"

"Yeah, I can handle that."

"Your name. What's your name?"

He peered at her through bloodshot eyes. "Name's John. John McDowel."

"John, are you married? Do you have a family?"

"Married? No, my wife left long ago. I have a daughter."

"Oh! … John, I want you to relax and warm up while we're in here. You know, I feel concerned about you." She took a sip of her coffee, wondering how best to tell him what was on her mind without getting him angry. But tell him she must. "John, how do you feel?"

He looked at her, surprised, almost incredulous that she should be asking such a question. "I'm fine! I'm fine!"

For the first time, though bloodshot, she noticed his blue eyes. "John, I can't and won't leave you until I say something about your drinking. Look at what happened to you. You could have been killed by that … that person who stole your wallet. He could have bopped you on the head and killed you. Drinking always leads to trouble. You really should stop. Also, there's help out there, if you want to quit, that is. And what about your daughter? How does she feel about the drinking?"

He looked down at his coffee. "Emily? She don't like it. She wants me to quit."

"Then why don't you? Do you have any idea how you're hurting her? "Try to imagine what it's like to have a father who drinks. Just try and put yourself into her shoes. John, you're giving her nothing but pain. How could she be proud of you? Imagine a young girl getting married or already married, and having to tell her fiance, or husband, that her father is a drunk!"

He looked guilty, but said nothing.

Meanwhile Tanya, as if driven, forged ahead with her reprimand.

Across the table from her, John sat mesmerized with his eyes barely moving from her face, his coffee untouched.

It was sometime later that Tanya suddenly remembered her job. She stopped in the middle of a sentence. "John, I've got to go!" She glanced at her watch with alarm. "It's ten already, and I'm two hours late."

He nodded.

"John, I have to go to work … like right now! But could you give me your address and a phone number before I leave?"

"Do you really want to know? I live by myself in a rooming house."

"Yes, I want to know. I'd like to check up on you to see if you're okay."

She found a pad of paper and handed him a pen. "Write on this. Write down your daughter's name and phone number, as well. And John, I'm going to give you my phone number and address because I'll be calling to see how you're doing."

She noticed that the address he put down wasn't too far from where the restaurant was.

Tanya rummaged through her purse and took out some money. "John, I want you to have this in case you need bus fare, or something to eat, especially since you were robbed last night."

She held out her hand to him. "Good bye, John. I'm sure by now everybody will be wondering where I am, so I've got to get to work. But I'll keep in touch, you may be sure. And don't think that I won't because I will."

As soon as Tanya walked into the office, she went directly to see George Fowler, her boss. She was his secretary. She wondered what he'd say to her. He was a young man, about fifteen years her junior. He was happily married and drew a terrific salary.

George looked up, surprised to see her.

"George, I'm so sorry I'm late. I stopped to help someone on my way to work. A kind of gentleman derelict. He was lying on the sidewalk. It was very sad because a lot of people saw him but they just walked around him, as if he didn't exist. Nobody was decent enough to ask why he was lying there, so I did."

As she told her story, she noticed that George had a strange look on his face. She thought she noticed tears. He seemed moved to tears by what she'd said.

"It's okay, Tanya. It's okay, don't worry about it," he kept reassuring her. He got to his feet, hurriedly.

Tanya stopped, seeing him brush a hand over his eyes. All that morning, she thought about George and his reaction when she'd told him why she was late.

Later she phoned Andy Clawk, a Salvation Army Supervisor that she happened to know. He kept track of all the different street people. She felt compelled to tell him about John.

"Andy, I thought it would be good to keep an eye on him. You know, call him to see how he's doing and things like that. He gave me his address and phone number, as well as his daughter's phone number. And if you find anything out, I want your promise that you'll call me."

"Tanya, I'd be very happy to do that. You certainly deserve to know." She was pleasantly surprised when he promptly phoned her that very afternoon.

"Tanya, I went to see John. He lives in an older house in a small suite. He invited me in. We sat down and had tea. And we had a very good talk. He told me that he was an alcoholic, which I kind of guessed already from what you said. He's a World War 11 veteran. But he's okay. He's okay. He said the reason he fell down was because he'd been drinking, and he was robbed because he was drunk."

"Andy, thank you for telling me. I really do appreciate this call. Thank you, so much. Do you think that now and then you could check up on him?"

"Tanya, it's not only my job, but my pleasure as well. I'll keep you posted whenever I do." They said good bye.

Four weeks later, Tanya received a letter from John McDowel.

Dear Tanya,

I stopped drinking after the lecture you gave me. You know you reminded me of my mother. She was the only one who cared enough for me to tell me not to drink. It's been four weeks and I'm still sober. Can you believe that?

I'm very happy that I met you. One morning I woke up and I met an angel. I saw an angel looking down on me. It was you. The angel was you. From that day on you changed my life. I phoned my daughter and I told her about you. I told her I stopped drinking. She's happy for me.

I'm thankful and I like it that you helped me and that we met. You know I'm glad you scolded me about the drinking. I needed that kind of talk to straighten myself out. Thank you for your help. As long as I live I'll never forget you.

Sincerely, John McDowel

Tanya sat smiling to herself while pondering over his letter. What a miracle that he'd changed so much! Alcoholics rarely stop drinking on their own. She knew that John could do that only if he'd had God's grace to help him and depend on. Glory to God! Tanya went to show Walter the letter.

Later she called Andy Clawk. "Have you had any contact with John?" She wanted to know.

"John? Yes, I went to see him several times and I'm glad to report that he's doing a hundred percent. Tanya, thanks to you he's happy and he's doing really well. And the good part, no more drinking."

"Andy, thanks. It's so good to hear."

It was music to her ears. She hung up the phone, grateful that she'd made such a difference in the life of a stranger.

THE END

PETER'S JOURNEY

Peter Moroz followed the other men to a small pub in London, England. Their large transport had landed after completing a flight into Germany. Europe was being rebuilt and their mission was to fly supplies into Berlin. Like himself the crew were mostly Canadians. It was 1949, and thank God the war was over. He'd signed on to help load and unload cargo. Sometimes he folded parachutes, and sometimes whatever was required of him. He liked the work and never complained.

He'd given up on school after Grade ten thinking that it was boring, a waste of time, especially since he could be earning money by joining the Air Force. There had been odd jobs which earned him enough money to buy beer and cigarettes. However, he felt restless, unfulfilled. He was only nineteen when he'd decided to join up. Why not make a career out of it? The pay was good. He didn't mind hard work. Here was a chance to see the world, to experience adventure, to gain respect from his peers, his family. And women, there were plenty of women who took notice of his handsome face. He was tall with a shock of dark hair, smooth perfect features and blue eyes. Three years later he found his job to be every bit as exciting as he'd always imagined it would be.

Now he entered the pub, eager to draw on a cigarette and a foaming glass of stout. Between flights the crew usually went for drinks. Peter enjoyed the relaxed, comforting feeling that drink gave him even if the feeling didn't last. Not long after that, in the same pub, he met an attractive English girl, Madge Higgens. Madge was beautiful. She had honey colored hair, a flawless skin and a smile that sent his heart racing every time he looked at her. They were introduced by the pilot who happened to know her.

"I like your accent," he'd said. "It's so English."

She'd laughed. "And yours ... uh... so Canadian."

They began dating. She brought him home to meet her widowed mother. After that Peter could think of nothing but Madge. She was a nurse who worked at one of the hospitals. Each time he was on a mission, he couldn't wait to get back to her. His love for her grew stronger, especially when he was away. It was then he decided to propose marriage. The thought that some other man might find her beautiful had helped him decide.

One day, as they sat in the pub where they'd first met, he took her hand and raised it to his lips. His blue eyes looked intensely into hers. Not at all sure now of her answer, he found himself trembling. "Madge, honey, would you .... would you do me the honor of being my wife? Madge, I love you. I don't want to think of my life without you."

Her eyes lit up in surprise. "Peter, of course I'll marry you. I've been waiting for you to ask me."

She began planning her wedding. She chose a flowing, lace gown and carried a sprawling bouquet of flowers picked from her mother's garden. A long black velvet ribbon hung from the bouquet. Peter noticed with surprise that she'd tied a replica of a black cat at the end of the ribbon.

"It's tradition, honey," she'd explained when he'd asked her about it. "A bride on her way to the church must be on the look out for lucky omens. One of them is meeting a black cat, or a chimney sweep. It's supposed to bring "good luck" to the happy couple. Most English brides believe that," she told him.

"But why a black cat?" Madge was a nurse. She was sensible, practical, not given to superstition.

"Because every bride carries one on her wedding day."

Peter smiled, thinking that no bride in Canada would be caught dead with a black cat anywhere near her, let alone tied to her wedding bouquet. However, if Madge believed in it and thought it was good luck, it was okay with him.

"Madge, honey, there's just one thing we have to discuss. I thought we should discuss it soon … now. … Uh-h-h, I'd like us to live in Canada, if you don't mind leaving England. You know I live in Edmonton. It's where I live. Uh-h-h, it's a city in the province of Alberta. I think you'd like it. And my brothers and sisters, they live there too." He added the last to solidify his request as if he couldn't live anywhere else. He caught her hand and looked entreatingly at her.

"But Peter, what about my mother!" Tears clouded her eyes.

"I know, I know. We could visit often ... you know my work permits me to fly anywhere."

His words calmed her. She sighed, dreading about having to tell her mother.

Peter, gentle, charming, kind, didn't want to make an issue of it. He wasn't quite sure what he'd have done had she said "no."

They made a handsome couple. He imagined bringing her home, knowing that his brothers, Martin and Anton, as well as his three sisters, would more that approve of her.

After the wedding they returned to Canada just as he'd hoped. He continued working for the Air Force. He drank more. He loved a party, or any kind of celebration as long as it involved drinks.

It was several years before they had a family. For Peter, those were restless years ... even boring. He suggested that they move to Las Vegas. Several times they'd landed there to pick up supplies. The gambling, the tall leggy women serving free drinks held a fascination for him. He found himself flirting with more than one beauty. He felt good knowing that he could still draw women to himself. One day, he confided his longings about the move to Madge. "Honey, I know you'll love it there," he assured her.

She agreed to the move. Madge found a large, airy furnished apartment, fairly cheap and close to The Strip. It was exactly what Peter wanted. For the first while things went well for them. In between flights, they gambled and ate at the casinos. However, it didn't take long before their spending outgrew his income. The rent began to pile up as well as unpaid bills. Eventually what Peter was dreading happened. They received an eviction notice. It was then they decided to move back to Edmonton.

Madge returned to nursing. They needed the money.

The years went by and Madge gave birth to five children, taking time off from her job for each child. Peter, well addicted by now, couldn't stop drinking even for the sake of his beloved family. Still, as each child was born he promised Madge that he'd taken his last drink. "Honey, trust me, this time I'm going to quit, I ... I promise, honey," he vowed, distraught by the look on her face, so serious, so upset. She was anxious that he keep his word. In his arms he held their latest child, a girl. "You bet I'll stop, hon. Look what I've got to inspire me."

His brother Martin, who'd come to see the baby, frowned. "Pete, it's about time you got off your ass and did something about the boozing. What about the kids? What kind of a Dad are you? And Madge, you mean to say she has to work so you can drink?... Pete, you ain't no husband. I'd have kicked your ass out long ago if I was her." Now he looked at Peter with scorn, not caring that Madge was present and listening.

Peter looked away, thinking that he didn't want to fight with Martin. Martin could be tough. He wouldn't forgive easily unless he really did stop the drinking. But could he? He'd tried several times, once he'd gone as long as a three months only to start up again thinking that just one more wouldn't matter because he could control it. Now he looked Martin square in the eye. "Okay, okay, I'll stop."

"You better. Me, if I were Madge, ... I wouldn't give you anymore chances. I'd throw you out! Yeah, that's what I'd do, ... throw you out."

He hung his head. "Okay Martin, yeah, I see what you mean." He could have said something in his own defense, but he didn't want to stir Martin up any further.

Later Anton showed up. He wasn't as blunt as Martin had been. His concern was not only for Madge and the children, but for Peter's health and he questioned him closely. "So how are you doing? Are you, uh-h-h, looking for work? Uh-h-h, how are you feeling?"

He nodded. "Yeah, I'm okay, ... yeah, really am okay." He knew that though Anton was worried about the drinking, he wouldn't embarrass him in front of Madge. Not the way Martin had done.

For the sake of his growing family, Peter stopped drinking. Wherever his job took him, if they hit a bar, he ordered coffee or ginger ale. The men teased him about it, making it difficult to keep his promise to Madge. Staying sober wasn't easy. Several months passed before he started sneaking drinks again. However, he tried to keep the drinking down only to weekends. But as soon as Martin found out, his anger flared up and he no longer trusted anything Peter said.

Peter tried winning him back. Weren't they brothers? Doesn't one forgive?

It did no good, Martin's mind was made up. "Pete, you ain't gonna change, I know that for sure now." His eyes spoke contempt.

The children, three girls and two boys were a handful to raise. But Peter, whenever he was home was always there for them, loving, caring, listening. If it wasn't for the drinking, he would have been the most perfect husband and father a woman could want.

However, not long after that Madge's patience ran out and she soon tired of his broken promises.

Many times his job kept him away from home for as long as a week. It didn't help their marriage.

Her face somber, she warned him again and again. "Peter, about the drinking, if you don't stop you give me no choice, I'll have to divorce you. ... Yes, divorce you. I don't want to live like this. I can support myself quite well. Uh-h-h, but you'll have to help support the children."

He froze. "Support the children? He didn't like upheavals. "Madge, I'm sorry, honey. I can change. But the children, I'll never see them if you divorce me. You do believe I can change don't you?" He was shaking.

She sighed. "To be honest, it's for the sake of our children that I want you to leave.... You're not a good role model. They'll grow up thinking that drinking is a way of life."

For several months, Peter tried to stop. But each time he was away from Madge, he made no attempt to quit. She found out soon enough when he arrived home drunk one evening.

She frowned and wouldn't allow him to kiss her. "Peter, you've had plenty of chances. I can't have you coming home drunk. Especially in front of the children. This is it. Out!"

"Plenty of chances? Madge, do you mean that you want me to leave?"

"Yes, I do." She looked determined.

Reluctantly, he had to admit that she was right and accepted that she was actually throwing him out. Had Martin said something behind his back? No, Martin wouldn't interfere. And the drinking, well, he still hadn't licked it.

Martin was furious. "Pete, you're a damn fool. Know something? I would never desert my family for a drink. Pete, you should have your head examined. ... I mean it! And Madge, she should be given a medal for the years of crap she's had to put up with because of you!"

Martin's words dug into him. It was all too true and he knew it. The blow came the day he had to sign the divorce papers. Had it really come to this? Madge was very understanding about the visitation rights, and even encouraged him to come often. "The children still need a father," she reasoned.

His insides turned as sadness struck him. Tears blinded his eyes. It was spring. The time of year he liked best. What a shame to spoil it. He signed the papers, vowing that he would clean himself up and return to his family, sober. He embraced each child and kissed each goodbye. He and Madge parted as friends. He wouldn't have it any other way.

That evening, alone in a motel room with cigarette in hand and lying on his bed, he drank gin straight out of a bottle while agonizing over circumstances that he couldn't change or perhaps he could, had he had enough will power to do so.

Spring merged into summer. Peter, now on vacation, left the city planning to find work in Andrew, a small town that his mother came from. As he drove along the country road, the air was heady with the smell of wild roses, ripening wheat, and lush green grass that sprouted on both sides of the road. He breathed deeply, the fragrance filling his lungs, while reminding himself that he did have some relatives there.

Aunts, uncles, cousins, he went to see all of them, hoping someone would hire him. The support payments that he'd agreed to pay Madge were quite hefty and most of his salary from the Air Force went to Madge. Because it was the right thing to do and he loved his family, he didn't begrudge her even one penny.

Each relative he visited welcomed him warmly. However, except for a few odd jobs, there wasn't anything steady. Though he worked hard, he was let go from place to place as soon as the work was finished.

One day a heavy rain settled in, and he found himself with no work, no place to stay and nothing to do. He opened his wallet and counted the cash, then drove into town and parked in front of the Andrew Hotel, thinking it just possible that he'd run into one of the relatives who might hire him. He went straight for the beer parlor. Peter recognized some of the farmers that he'd worked for and made his way towards the bar. However, none of his relatives were in there.

"Three beers, please."

The bartender brought him his order which he downed quickly, while assuring himself that he still had plenty of money for a motel. He turned to a heavy set man sitting next to him. "Hey, Ed, you don't know of anyone who needs an extra hand, do you?"

"Are you kidding ? In this rain?"

"I don't mean now, I mean when it stops."

"Another round Mister?" It was the bartender.

He smiled. "Yeah, sure, bring me another."

So it began again, round after round, until all the money he'd saved for the motel was nearly gone. When the bar closed he got up, swayed towards the 1977 Buick sedan and started the motor. The condition he was in, he couldn't impose himself on any relatives.

Peter remembered a camp site on the edge of town. It was a good a place as any, he thought. He kept the motor running just long enough to heat the interior of the car then shut it off, afraid that he'd run out of gas, or asphyxiate himself. He found a blanket, crawled into the back seat and fell asleep.

Low on cash, he spent the summer drinking at the hotel evenings and sleeping at the campsite nights. It was most fortunate that every month he could still count on a check from the Air Force to make ends meet. However, thankfully with his vacation almost over, he was looking forward to getting back to a steady job of loading and unloading freight onto one of the airlines.

He was content that in spite of the drinking, he always managed to save enough to send to Madge. Summer gave way to fall and at the first sign of frost he decided to return to the city.

He went to see Madge and the children. There was so much he wanted to say. He noticed that his boys had grown, his three teenaged daughters looked more mature than he'd remembered. He looked at Madge. She looked older. There were some wrinkles that he hadn't seen before. "Honey, I must say that new hair style really suits you."

"Thank you, Peter."

His face sobered. Looking hopeful, he began, "Uh-h-h, how about us, hon, is there a chance that you've changed your mind?"

She looked away. "I don't think so. Not unless you've changed ... and I don't think you have."

He reached into his pocket for a cigarette, knowing that she was right. It was hard to be so close to those he loved. He tried to conceal his shaking hands from Madge. That evening he tried calling Martin to square things with him. However, other than a rude comment about his drinking, Martin wasn't too kind. He hung up, wishing he hadn't called.

The next morning he said good bye to his family and left for Crows Nest Pass in British Columbia. Why he'd chosen that destination, he wasn't really sure. Madge, the children and the support payments kept hammering at him. He had to keep working to keep those payments going.

It was nearly 11:00 P.M. when he registered at the Crow's Nest Hotel. He'd noticed a liquor store at the corner of the block and went to find it. The woman at the cash register was young, pretty, very friendly. She caught sight of Peter's handsome face and smiled at him. He returned the smile.

Madge had been clear about cutting ties with him. Was there someone else already in the picture? It made him wonder? What did he have to lose? Peter looked at the girl and and introduced himself. "I know this is kind of short notice, but u-h-h, would you like to join me for a drink?" he asked.

She responded readily. "Yes, I'd love to. I get off kinda late, though. ... Uh-h-h, twelve, if that's okay with you. My name is Barbie."

"Yeah, okay. I'm staying at the hotel. You know ... just down the street. Twelve you said? I'll come back then."

He went back to the hotel, thinking that he'd just picked up a woman and knew in advance that it would be a one night stand. Something he hadn't done since leaving Madge.

After that night, Peter's role changed from father and husband to philanderer. At one point, to promote a cruise, he went on a cruise to the Caribbean with a woman that he'd met at a cocktail party. Not only did she drink, but she couldn't stop talking. He was glad to be rid of her when the cruise ended.

The years went by. Whenever he could he always checked on Madge and his family. It hurt to find out that Madge was having a relationship with a wealthy stock broker. The day he found out about it he was struck with burning jealousy. He'd caught a plane to Ottawa to see her and the children.

"My mother did move here," she explained. "She wanted to be closer to the grandchildren."

Madge was still very beautiful, her figure slim, her hair as blonde as he'd remembered it. She looked happy, content. He wished she wasn't.

He nodded, hoping that the hurt wouldn't show in his eyes and forced himself to sit down and behave rationally. "Madge, how about dinner?"

"Why I'd love to," she consented readily. "Uh-h-h, thought you should know that I've met someone. Thomas. He ... I ... uh-h-h, we're going to Florida for a vacation. He's asked me to marry him."

He couldn't speak. He wished his smile was more real, so he nodded in acceptance.

They chose a Chinese restaurant. Madge loved Chinese food. He pretended to be indifferent to whatever was occurring in her life. When he left, he was thankful that he hadn't made a fool of himself, thankful that he hadn't broken down and wept, thankful that he hadn't asked if she'd take him back. In his heart he knew he hadn't a chance with her. After some time, he told himself that he really had no right to be jealous, remembering the kind of husband he'd been. Then remembering Carla, he thought of the immoral, nomadic life he was living at present.

Carla was a realtor and an accountant. She was intelligent and very good with numbers. She was a single parent, divorced with two grown children, a boy and a girl. "My husband had an affair with his secretary, so we separated. The bastard! Good enough reason for you?" She'd explained when he'd inquired about her status after meeting her.

Peter smiled, nodded, and lifted her hand to his lips. Carla was blonde, with a good figure, much more voluptuous than Madge's. He sensed her aggressiveness. Madge was of a gentler disposition.

They met at a party. At the time, he could see that she'd had more than enough to drink. Peter had driven her home. She didn't mind when he'd asked her if he could come in. At her suggestion, they spent the night together. Later, as she lay sleeping beside him, he was gripped with nostalgia remembering Madge. There was no doubt in his mind that he'd always love her. Was this to be her replacement?

He reached for a bottle of brandy beside the bed. It helped him forget about Madge and the children. ... His heart ached for the family that he'd given up. Did they miss him? What a pity that they couldn't reconcile. Sometimes he thought about Martin. Each time he returned home he tried calling him. But with Martin there was no forgiveness. Peter couldn't accept that Martin could be so hard on him, so cold towards him.

For several years they traveled. Carla's salary combined with his was more than enough to live on. All his children had married. He'd heard that Madge was still with Thomas. In his heart, Peter finally let her go.

He turned to Carla. She was a great partner, she was fun. They lived from one vacation to the next. They flew to Europe, Australia, Hawaii. Carla loved to party as much as he did. She liked to drink. She suited him. He couldn't have asked for a better companion.

One morning he rose from their bed and shuffled into the bathroom, feeling as if he'd lost weight. For certain his pants felt looser. I can do with some weight loss, he told himself, tightening the belt on his pyjamas. He examined himself in the mirror. One would scarcely recognize him from his youth. His face was lined and the permanent redness of the skin was there to stay. His body shape, beginning from his shoulders, had gradually expanded to a very wide girth. It wasn't something that he was proud of, remembering how slim he'd once been. How handsome! The change shocked him. Now he was far from good looking.

The smoking, drinking, the fast food had left their mark. He never was one to take care of himself and at sixty eight he was at least fifty pounds over. Several times he'd felt chest pains. Lately he'd noticed a drop in energy. He stepped on the scale. Two hundred and twenty-seven pounds. A drop of three pounds without even trying. He came back to bed where Carla was still sleeping. Reaching out, he gently ran his hand over her smooth cheek. It would have been nice if they'd married.

She opened her eyes and looked at him. "Peter, honey, what's wrong? You look so ... so, serious."

"I think I'll see Dr. Mayfair this week. Need a check up."

"Is something wrong?" she asked, already worried.

"Course not. Just routine."

She let it drop and pulled him down next to her. How could she love someone as misshapen as himself? he wondered. Later in the afternoon he went to see the doctor. Dr. Mayfair knew about his drinking habits.

"I want blood samples ... uh-h-h, and chest x-ray. We'll check your liver. I don't like your color. It's too sallow."

He heard from the doctor the next day. "The x-ray shows a spot on your liver. We'll have keep an eye on it. And one more thing, I've requested an ultra sound of your heart. The tests from the ECG indicate some blockage. I want to be sure." There was a lengthy pause. "Pete, if I'm right, you'll need bypass surgery. I'll see that you get a good surgeon. Uh-h-h, and one more thing, it should be done as soon as possible."

He felt himself pale. So it was serious. I'll tell Carla, he thought, but only as little as possible. No sense in worrying her.

Carla was shocked when he told her the news. She smiled through her tears. "It can't be. I won't let you be sick."

"Honey I'm sorry, but please don't worry. I''ll be all right. I just know it. Most people recover from a bypass." He put his arms around her, still very optimistic in his thinking.

Two weeks later, Peter's bypass was done by a Dr. Reed at the University Hospital. He didn't tell anyone in his family. He preferred they think of him as the strong, virile person he'd always been. Though he had to admit that he felt very weak and nothing like his old self.

Carla was there every day, laughing, talking nonsense, making him wish he was home and recovering in his own bed. It was November 11, 1999. Armistice Day. He knew that some of the men he'd worked with before retiring would be celebrating in some bar.

Dr. Reed entered the room. "Pete, no more drinking. Your heart and liver can't take it. Stay off the liquor. Weak? You say you're weak? Well, the tests show that your liver is damaged."

It shocked him, he couldn't imagine not having the strength he'd had before. He was discharged shortly after, though still only partly recovered. Carla was at his side helping him dress and guiding him to the bathroom.

Six weeks later, he went back to the hospital for a checkup. Dr. Reed held his x-rays up to the light for him to see. "Pete, there's something you should know. Your heart is still very weak. Uh-h-h, it's beating much slower than normal. That could account for the lack of energy. With time and exercise it might improve. We'll just have to wait and see."

He nodded, speechless, while trying to cope with the effect of his words. Another shock! Could he adjust to being only half well? He thought the bypass would fix everything. Another change, his voice. Now he could barely speak above a whisper. It bothered him to have to repeat himself even to Carla.

He phoned Martin one day to tell him about the surgery. However Martin, though he listened to him, wasn't impressed and didn't comment. He hung up the phone, wondering if Martin was still holding a grudge against him? Then he decided to visit Anton, though still not too steady on his feet. Perhaps it was the weight. He noticed that he was down another 20 pounds.

Anton and Anna were both happy to see him. When he left he felt buoyed by the visit. It felt good to forget about his heart, to laugh, to be normal. September was almost over and there was a pungent smell of autumn in the air. He breathed deeply, hoping that everything would turn out well for him.

Once home, he reached for a bottle of brandy.

Carla frowned "Pete, you're not supposed to have any ... the doctor told you that."

"Carla, I was only going to have one glass. ... It might even do me some good, you know." But he put the bottle down and reached for the paper instead.

He opened his eyes to look at the clock on the night stand. 4:30 A.M. He pushed back the covers and slowly lowered his feet to the floor. A wave of dizziness washed over him. Peter gathered his strength and heaved his weight up, before blackness engulfed him.

He awoke with a paramedic applying oxygen to his mouth. Once in the ambulance, Carla held his hand until they reached the hospital. "Honey, it's going to be all right," he assured her, wanting to replace her concern with a smile.

"What happened?" she whispered

"Honey, I was so weak, I couldn't stand. I think I blacked out."

"Yes, that was it. But why?"

"I wish I knew."

Again the doctor took several chest x-rays, but there was nothing significant about his condition that could be treated. "The bypass looks okay," he told him.

By now Peter was hooked up to oxygen, a catheter, a feeding tube and a heart monitor. Every time he tried to move, weakness took hold. He told himself it was only something temporary.

Anton came to visit him in the afternoon.

Peter turned to ask, "has anyone told Martin that I'm in here?"

"I'm sure Carla has. She phoned us." Anton stayed only a short while. Peter could see that he was deeply worried.

Several days later he wasn't much better. Carla had been in to see him in the morning. Though always an optimist, he now felt overwhelmed by feelings of hopelessness, despair and depression. He wondered how much longer he'd have to endure being chained to this bed before he was well enough to go home.

Peter, deep in glum thoughts, became aware that someone was standing beside his bed. He turned to look. It was Martin. A sudden feeling of joy swept through him. "Martin! Martin! Where have you been? Were you never going to speak to me again, Martin?"

Martin's face creased into a smile. Tears flooded his eyes. He wiped them away and looked down. "Pete, I never expected to see you like this." He bent down and put his arms around his brother. "Pete, I love you. ... I'm sorry this happened to you. Pete, so sorry."

Such a feeling of elation spread through Peter that he could hardly contain himself. Now he was sure that everything would be all right for him. "Martin, ... I missed you Martin! I'm so glad you came. You don't know what you've done for me by coming here. Martin, I feel so much better already." He forced himself up, slightly.

"Pete, I didn't know you were in this ... this kind of condition. Carla only phoned me today." His voice tapered off into uncertainty.

"But Martin, I did phone you, I did! You wouldn't listen even when I told you I had the bypass." He felt definitely stronger.

Martin couldn't take his eyes off him. He hadn't seen his brother for a long time. It was shocking to see him so emaciated.... only a shell of his former self. A feeling of sorrow and regret gripped him for the time lost when they could have enjoyed each others' company. Peter liked to laugh, to focus on the bright side of life. Martin suddenly realized that because of his judgmental, stubborn attitude, he'd missed a lifetime of his brother's giving nature, his kindness, his love for anyone he happened to know. Was it too late?

Martin sat by his bedside, with a hand resting on his arm, until Peter grew too weary to speak. "Pete, I'll be back tomorrow. See you then." He leaned over and kissed him on his forehead.

Peter grinned and for a second, Martin glimpsed a shadow of his handsome good looks despite the wrinkles that lined his face. "Martin, thanks for coming. I mean it. ... So, glad you came."

He fell asleep, as Martin was leaving. He awoke the next morning feeling better than he'd felt since the bypass. It was a miracle. His voice was stronger.

Now Martin came to see him every day to make up for lost time. One by one the oxygen, catheter, and intravenous tubes were removed. Peter began to walk, though slowly, to the bathroom by himself. His doctor was amazed at this sudden burst of strength from a patient he thought he was losing. "Keep this up and I'll have to send you home," he told him.

"Doc, today I feel the best yet. ... It's like I'm on top of the world."

It had to do with Martin forgiving him, with Martin expressing his love for him, with Martin caring enough to come to see him. He'd been hurt ... deeply hurt by Martin's rejection. It seemed the guilt of his drinking, separating from Madge and not having looked after her and his children had been swept away.

Carla came to pick him up at the hospital several days later. Peter, though weak, felt elated. He was going home. "Honey, I never thought I'd leave this hospital. Just think, tonight with you beside me, I'll sleep in my own bed."

Carla smiled as she helped him into the van. "Peter, it's so good that you're coming home. ... I missed you. Are you sure you're better?"

"Yes Carla! Honey, next week it's my birthday. What a present!"

Outside the sun warmed the cool October morning. He noticed the trees with the leaves blown off and lying in soft mounds on the ground. Children playing inside a school yard. Overhead, a vapor trail streamed through the sky. He was reminded of his job. He thought it was all so beautiful, so precious. Life was precious.

"Honey, we're here." Carla stopped the car in the driveway.

He unbuckled his seat-belt and slowly slid to the pavement. Carla put an arm around his waist and walked him to the door. Once inside, he hugged her, as tears gathered and came spilling down his cheeks. He wiped them away while Carla steered him toward the bedroom. "Come, lie down. You need to rest."

Suddenly, he realized that he might not make it to the bed. He sagged to the edge. "Sorry, honey, I'm still weak."

She helped him undress and get into pyjamas. Gratefully he lay down, pulled the covers over his chest and closed his eyes.

He was up in an hour. It was nearly noon. Pushing back the covers, he thought he should find Carla and sat up. He felt lightheaded and was conscious of his heartbeat which seemed very slow. Step by step, he carefully made his way to the kitchen.

Carla was making sandwiches for lunch. "Hi, honey how are you? Did you sleep?"

"Yes. ... Uh-h-h, I hate to say this, but actually I'm feeling not too good. ... You know, weak."

She looked alarmed. "Peter, what's wrong?"

"I don't know, but I can't seem to catch my breath. ... For some reason, I'm really sweating."

"I'll call an ambulance." She reached for the phone.

He sighed. The very last thing he wanted was to return to the hospital. But how could he help it? Perhaps it was indigestion and he'd be back that very day. A feeling of dread gripped him. In no time the doorbell was ringing and the ambulance was there. He opened the door to find two attendants with a gurney. Carla was at his side.

"This is my husband, ... uh-h-h, he's having trouble with his breathing." She'd called him "husband." Many times he'd wished it was so.

One of the paramedics helped him onto the stretcher. Peter held out his hand to Carla. "Honey, could you?" He smiled at her, as she took his hand.   Suddenly his face lit up. A soft glow spread over his features. "I see a light. It's so bright! So bright! Slowly he let go of Carla's hand. His fingers uncurled. Now his eyes became transfixed on a light that only he could see. He sighed deeply, as his breath expelled all at once. Peter's head and body went limp. His eyes glazed over. Carla gently pulled her hand away. "God rest his soul, he's at peace," she said. "Perfect peace."

THE END

THE LANGUAGE OF LOVE

Tanya looked out at the seagulls swooping over a rolling ocean. Overhead the sky was an azure blue with banks of fluffy clouds ever in motion. She turned to Walter. "Walter, it's such a beautiful day. But Hawaii is beautiful every day, isn't it? I'm glad we took this trip. Walter, let's go for a walk, you know, by the Ala Wai canal."

Walter got up from his chair on the balcony of their rented suite at The Banyon Hotel. "Yeah, you're right, I could use some exercise. Ala Wai did you say? Well, why not? Get your runners on."

The canal, which ran through Waikiki was built to drain the rice paddies and swamps shortly after the city started to grow. The many swamps had been drained to rid the city of infected Aedes mosquitoes which carried dengue fever. After draining the canal, the area in Waikiki became a major tourist resort that it is today.

The Ala Wai always has a plentiful supply of fish, shrimp and crabs to be caught. However, nothing should be eaten from its waters due to the pollutants draining from the streets, especially lead from gasoline use. Once a giant Mantis Shrimp was found burrowing in the shallow muck of the canal. Surprisingly, it had grown to 15 inches and weighed in at 1.35 pounds.

It was mid-morning and the sun was still tolerable. The Kushinsky's were on a two week holiday. They'd come with family, Tanya's two sisters, and their husbands. All three couples were staying at the same hotel. However, this morning the two other couples had gone to the beach to suntan.

Tanya ran to catch up to Walter, who had stopped to watch a man reel in a fish at that very moment.

"Well look at that! Do you see how big it is? Looks like Tilapia! They're bottom feeders and there's quite a lot of them here, I noticed."

Tanya nodded. "I've never seen them that large. But you know there are signs all over warning people not to eat the fish because the waters are so polluted. I wonder why anyone would take such a chance? They say there's zinc, copper and super nutrients in the run off that ends up in the canal. The fish love it and that's why they grow to such a tremendous size. "

There was a warm breeze blowing that morning as they turned and took up a brisk pace along the sidewalk that ran parallel to the narrow stretch of water. So pleasant, so delightful, Tanya thought remembering the snow and below zero temperatures they'd left in Edmonton, Alberta, where they'd lived most of their lives. It was the beginning of

February and the actual thaw wouldn't start until nearly the end of the month. Their vacation had been timed to shorten the long, cold winter.

The only thing Tanya really missed was St. Edmunds Catholic Church where she often led the congregation as lead singer.

As they walked along, Tanya looked up to see a little boy sitting on the grass by the sidewalk. He seemed to be alone with nobody close by watching him. "Walter look, he's crying. Let's stop and ask him if he's all right. Maybe he's lost."

Walter knelt down and took the child's hands in his. "Uh-h-h, Son, why are you sitting here crying? What's wrong?"

The boy, no more than six, still sobbing turned to look at Walter. He had black hair and slanted eyes, for certain he was Asian. He answered in a strange language that neither Walter or Tanya understood.

"I think that's Japanese, Walter."

"Yeah, I think you're right." He looked into the child's eyes. "What's your name? Can you tell us your name?" Walter spoke slowly trying to communicate with the boy, hoping that he knew some English.

Again the boy answered in Japanese.

No matter what Walter said, the boy spoke to him in Japanese, or they assumed it was Japanese.

"Tanya, it's too bad we have no cell phone, but somehow we're going to have to get hold of the police and they'll have to handle it. He's definitely lost. But he must have parents or someone who cares for him, somewhere. He doesn't look neglected.… You know, we could go to McDonalds,… You know the one across from the beach? They'd have a phone there and they could contact the police for us."

Walter rose from a kneeling position and stood up. "Come."

The boy, with his hand clinging to Walter's hand, stood up. By now he'd stopped crying, and with childish innocence, with his trust focused entirely on Walter, he obediently followed Walter and Tanya in the direction of the beach. Not once did he let go of Walter's hand. Tanya noticed that he didn't respond as readily to her as he did to Walter.

"Walter, his Dad must be some role model because he's set on holding on to you. Have you noticed that?"

Walter nodded. "Yeah."

As soon as they reached McDonald's, Walter determined to speak to someone, stopped a young man who worked there. "Excuse me, we found this little boy crying, he's probably lost his parents. Does anybody here speak Japanese? He doesn't speak English."

The young man shook his head. "Sorry, no one here that I know of."

"I see. We have to find his parents. They must have reported him missing by now. Could you phone the police for me?"

"Yeah, sure thing. We'll get them for you." The young man produced a cell phone. He made the call and turned to Walter. "They're sending down a couple of officers. They said they'd be here in about ten."

Walter, with the boy at his side, stood looking out the window. In a short while a police car drew up and stopped at the curb. "They're here." Walter opened the door that led to the street.

A police officer got out of the cruiser and approached them. "This the boy? You say he's lost and you found him by the Ala Wai?"

"Yes, officer, we did. Do you speak Japanese? He doesn't speak English."

"Not me, but Officer Yamoto, he speaks Japanese."

The other officer got out of the car and came close to where the boy stood. He looked down at the boy and smiled, then said something to him in his own language. The boy answered the officer promptly in Japanese.

Officer Yamoto pointed to the cruiser, opened the door and held out his hand to the boy. The boy shook his head, said something to the officer, but he wouldn't budge and he wouldn't let go of Walter's hand, drawing away from the officer each time he spoke. Again the officer tried to coax the child to get into the cruiser. Finally he stopped.

Officer Yamoto, looking frustrated, turned to Walter. "Mr. Kushinsky, I think you, your wife and the boy, will have to come with us. It seems he won't get into the cruiser without you. I think we've found his parents. A report was turned in by a Japanese couple who claim to have lost their son. They're waiting for us at The Hilton."

Walter smiled. "I see. Okay. Tanya, let's go."

The three got into the cruiser with the boy holding tight to Walter. Walter, with the boy in the middle, and Tanya on the other side of him, settled into the back seat. Tanya, reflecting upon how the boy had already become attached to them, had to smile to herself.

In no time they were at The Hilton and getting out of the cruiser. With the two officers in the lead, they entered the luxurious, opulent setting of the hotel, filled with its tropical plants and gushing waterfalls.

The boy, pressed close to Walter, now stood uncertain.

Tanya's eyes went beyond the tables crowded with people and their chatter to the far end of the large room. Then she saw them and instantly knew who they were. A Japanese man and woman, the woman slight with dark hair, and dressed in a white dress. Suddenly, the woman came rushing toward the trio with her arms outstretched to claim her son. She stopped dead in front, then swooped the child up into her arms and crushed him to herself, murmuring something into his ear while showering him with kisses.

She turned to Walter and Tanya, bowing to each. "Thank you, thank you. You find my son. I so grateful to you. So grateful. Thank you, that you find him."

Walter and Tanya with tears in their eyes at the emotional reunion, stood smiling, happy that it had ended so well. The boy's father, a young man with Asian features, came forward smiling. He bowed slightly first to Walter, then to Tanya. Then he shook Walter's hand, then Tanya's. "My sincere thanks to both, that you find our son. Many thanks."

Walter turned to Tanya. "All the time he was with us, he wouldn't let go of my hand until he saw his mother. I'm really glad we found him. What a beautiful child. Shall we continue our walk?"

THE END

THE LIFE OF A PURSE

"Teresa, Merry Christmas, hope you like it."

"Martin, for me? … What a gorgeous purse!"

I held up the purse to examine it. "Wherever did you get it?"

"Uh-h-h, in one of the shops."

"Like it? I love it! And I'll put it to good use."

Actually, I thought it would be just the thing to carry my books in, to and from the University of Alberta where I was enrolled in Fine Arts.

As for Martin, my husband, he really had fine taste, I thought. A wide band went over the shoulder and down to the hips. It was shaped like a half moon and the material … a soft, black Italian leather.

There were many side pockets. I found pockets on top of pockets. It had many compartments, some with zippers, some just slits. You could hide something inside quite easily and never find it. In an emergency it could easily replace an overnight bag. It was quite in style and really the "in thing." I noticed the inside was lined with strong black cotton.

There was a card in one of the pockets with a price on it. Martin had paid $200.00 for the purse. Not cheap! He'd bought it at "Holt and Renfrew," a shop that catered to the well heeled. I took to it the minute I looked at it.

Though I was older than the regular run of students, I held my own academically at the university. Ever since Martin gave me the okay to attend, I was determined to secure an Arts degree and my determination resulted in better than average marks. There was a Chinese student in the class who wasn't doing as well as the others and I felt sorry for Chang, so whenever I could I put aside some time to review the lectures with him.

Three years later, to my satisfaction, he managed to pass all the finals when we graduated. I came through with honors. Martin, who worked in the medical field, though a tiny bit envious, had secretly predicted that I might drop out. Now he was quite proud that I'd made it and was bragging about it to all his friends.

That summer several students in my class went to Europe to view some of the finest art in the world.

"Martin, if you don't mind, I'd like to go with them. It's part of our curriculum," I explained to justify my reasons to him as well as to myself.

Martin thought it was okay if I went. He didn't seem to mind my going but he wasn't entirely sure that it should take a trip to Europe to enrich my knowledge of fine art. For me, it was a real thrill ... art, painting, music, they were my passions.

I had attended a Catholic School in my Junior High days and the year before I'd gone to New York with a couple of nuns. So just to be convincing, I told Martin I thought that the nuns would approve of the trip.

My four girls were old enough to look after the house and Martin didn't much care for the arts. So I packed my bags, threw my Italian leather purse over my shoulder and went along with the art group.

A week later, we were settled in a hotel in Rome. We had arrived on the weekend and I'd read about a symphony being held close by at an opera house. Why not attend, I thought.

Because it was a Sunday, I dressed in a sheer, periwinkle blue dress for the occasion, thinking that not many people would be dressed in jeans for such a classy event. I was kind of let down when I found out that no one from the Arts group was interested in coming with me.

In fact, Tristin, the girl I shared a room with, stared at me in disbelief. "Why would anyone want to go to a symphony in Rome? There are better things to do than that. And on a Sunday?"

"Fine, I'll go alone," I said, all the more set on going whether she came with me or not. However, I returned a short time later, disappointed. "Tristen, it's been canceled."

"Then why not come with us? We're all going to the market and they say it's like a field of shopping stalls over there."

She held my interest. "Shopping? Yes, I'll go." Another passion of mine. I snuggled my purse close to my side and went to test out the shopping. After all I still had to bring something back for my girls and Martin.

Once we got to the market there was such a crowd pressing in on every side it made me wish I'd stayed home. Even harder to keep together with the rest of the troupe.

I hung on to my purse possessively, remembering too late the warnings about leaving anything of value at the hotel. I looked around. There was no one but me even carrying a purse.

A group of young boys jostled past me. All of a sudden, I felt my purse sag. At the same time from the corner of my eye, I caught a glint of metal. My hand felt for the bag. I was anxious not to let it leave my side. It seemed intact, until I realized that my fingers were running over the lining and not the purse. I looked down. A wide slit in the leather gaped back at me. I felt a shock. In such a crowd I was really a mark! That knife could easily have cut through me and not just the purse. I felt my knees go weak. I touched Tristin's arm.

"Tristin stop! Look what's happened!" He ... they ... someone just ripped open my purse! I think with a knife. But he didn't cut through the lining. Thank God I still have everything! That's what saved me."

The others students looked on in disbelief when they saw the purse. Tristin shook her head. "Teresa, it's those clothes you're wearing. You're dressed much too fine for going to a market."

"I know. That's because I'm dressed for a symphony and not the market. When I returned I didn't have time to change."

Then and there everybody decided to go back to the hotel since the enthusiasm for shopping had died off.

As soon as I came home I showed Martin the purse.

"You can have it fixed. Be happy you weren't hurt."

"Yes, I could have been hurt."

The next day I took it to a shoemaker who did a fine job of sewing it together. It looked the same except that now it angled somewhat differently. However, my love for the purse still held and I continued to take it everywhere.

A year later I went to Montreal to visit Rebbeca, my daughter, who was attending McGill University. She had just finished a semester in music. I didn't tell her that I was coming since I thought it might be nice to surprise her.

When I got there, Rebbeca had a suggestion which I liked. "Mom, why don't we go to New York? Just the two of us. It would be fun, don't you think? We're not that far from there and we could look at some art galleries ... do some shopping ... okay?"

The minute Rebbeca said "art galleries" she had my interest. "You're right, I think that since I'm here already we might as well make the most of it."

We took a bus to New York, which wasn't too expensive. I packed only a few things because we planned to stay only the one night. Once in New York, we got down from the bus to face a drenching rain. I looked around in exasperation.

It was something we hadn't counted on. "We'll have to work around this rain. Right now, let's look for a hotel. You know, when I was here with the nuns, we stayed at a hotel close to the monastery. Let's try there."

"Anywhere, Mom, anywhere! We've got to get out of this downpour!"

I thought a minute. "On second thought, maybe not. Why? Because the hotel isn't exactly in the best part of town. Rebecca, I went there with the sisters and every day it was the same thing. We'd hear fighting in the street below. It was mostly transients fighting. I could actually hear the crunch of flesh as they went at it. One morning I looked out the window, and what did I see? It was them, the homeless, bashing each other around and making that awful crunching noise. This went on day after day after day. There was blood everywhere. Once I went down to check the sidewalk just to see for myself. It was covered with blood. Blood everywhere. You wouldn't want to stay there. Let's try someplace closer to down town."

"Mom, I know of a place. I've read about it, "The Aston". It's new, it's down town ...let's go."

Because of the rain, we took a cab to the hotel. The Aston was perfect. Our room was reasonable in price and very clean. We unpacked and since it was only noon, we decided to explore some of the shops.

Outside, it was still raining. However, rain or no rain, we were determined to see and do as much as we could in the one day. Without a moment's hesitation we stepped into the downpour, bobbing in and out of shops along the way to keep out of the wet. Our makeup was washed clean, our hair hung in dripping strands, my handbag took on a darker color of black as we darted from store to store until we were both starving hungry.

I turned to Rebbeca. "I can't go much longer, I'm starved! How about you? Well I shouldn't wonder, nearly three by my watch. We've had nothing to eat since breakfast."

"Okay, let's stop for lunch," Rebecca agreed.

We found a secluded restaurant not too far from our hotel. Though still early afternoon, it was full with quite a crowd in the dining room. The waiter brought us a menu and I ordered first.

"I'll have the cream of leak soup, crackers and fresh baked rolls."

"Mom, that sounds good. I'll have the same."

I took off my coat and put my purse on the floor next to the wall. Theft was quite common in the big city. Just to be safe, I pressed my foot against it.

"Rebbeca, after lunch let's go to Bloomingdale's. And how about the Metropolitan Museum? Isn't that why we came? I'd like to see that. And how about a live play? ... And that too."

Rebecca was game no matter what I suggested. We speeded up lunch, so I wrapped up a soft roll in a serviette and tucked it into my purse thinking that I'd eat it later.

Once more we started on the round of shops, so exciting, so different with neither one of us wanting to quit.

In Saks, we found a great display of cosmetics, beautifully co-ordinated in a rainbow of colors.

"Mom, you can get blush here exclusive for your coloring, They'll mix it special to suit your skin."

"Really? Let's have it done! ... Yes?"

When I reached into my purse to pay for the makeup, it pained me to see how very wet it was by then. And what an awful odor each time I opened it. I turned to Rebbeca. "You know, "New York doesn't smell all that great. Actually, it stinks! Even my purse smells bad. Is it the rain, the city, or what?

"Oh Mom, don't be so picky!"

I shut the purse as we ducked into another doorway. My clothes were beginning to stick to my body. Rain or no rain, we had no time to lose and a minute later we dashed out again at a good trot to Bloomingdales ... then Macy's. We checked out the plays. They were all sold out.

"Too bad. Let's eat." I looked at my watch. It was already after six and the shops were closing. We found a small restaurant, ordered dinner, then went back to the hotel.

The minute we got in I took off my wet clothes and showered. Both Rebbeca and I put on a bathrobe before stretching out on a luxurious cream colored bedspread.

"What a gorgeous room! And at such a good price! If your father knew what a bargain we got, I think he'd be proud of us." I nodded in satisfaction.

Rebbeca picked up the remote to turn on the television.

I reached for a satin pillow and buried my head into its softness, marveling at such luxury. I lay back about ready to succumb to a quick nap. Suddenly out of the corner of my eye I caught sight of something running across the carpet. Was it a mouse? I sat up, wondering should I tell Rebbeca or not? If I said one word, there would be a scene, screams, and who knows what else. A minute later it appeared again, this time running for my suitcase. There were some clothes piled on top. I shuddered. That was final straw!

"Rebbeca, I think we have a visitor."

Rebbeca looked up in alarm to examine the room. "What visitor? What are you talking about? I don't see anyone. Are you crazy?"

"I mean the four legged kind."

Rebbeca tensed and sat up. . "Four legged kind? What do you mean?"

"I mean I saw a mouse!"

Her voice picked up in volume. She screamed out, "A mouse? What do you mean a mouse? What'll we do?" She drew up her feet in revulsion. "Call the concierge downstairs and tell him. Quick! You'll have to do it, I'm too scared."

I made the call. "We have a mouse in our room," I said.

Thomas, the concierge, corrected me. "No, you can't have. This is one of the finest hotels in New York. It's unheard of!"

"May we suggest that you might want to come up and check our room."

"Yes, ma'am, I'll be right up."

A minute later and he was in our room and looking around. "You have a problem? Did you say you saw a mouse in this room? I'm sorry, I don't believe it."

"But I did see … " I got no further as a ratty, cinnamon colored mouse crept out from under my suitcase. The hair on its back looked unbelievably scruffy and packed down. It streaked for the bathroom.

Suddenly Thomas went white. With one lunge, he leaped onto my bed. I followed him in quick succession, then Rebbeca.

Rebbeca let out scream after scream as the three of us stood rocking and leaning forward to see where the mouse had gone.

The concierge turned to look at us. "Well, I never!" he muttered, before gingerly getting off the bed when he realized that he'd have to use the phone to call the desk. "This is most unusual! Most unusual! I'll get someone up here right away."

Rebbeca and I slowly came off the bed. I pointed to the bathroom. "He's in there."

We approached the bathroom cautiously, ready to bolt should the mouse make its appearance. After a quick examination, Thomas turned to us. "I'll get you another room. Sorry I didn't believe you. But it's never happened before. From the looks of him, it's one of those garbage mice you might find in a garbage can."

He moved us to yet a nicer room than the one we had. "It's too bad we're leaving tomorrow," I said to Rebbeca. She agreed that it was.

Martin was waiting for me at the airport when I flew in from Montreal. I took off my purse and dropped it to the floor.

"It's good to be home," I told him. "New York was okay, but it rained all the time we were there. And this purse, I don't know what's happened to it, but it's picked up the most awful smell you can imagine."

"Sorry to hear that. It was an expensive purse." Martin nodded, and went to turn on the television.

I hoisted the bag up and spilled the contents onto the dining room table. I was anxious to clean it and shed the odor. First I opened all the zippered compartments then shook out the purse. I was surprised to see the serviette, with my bun still in it, roll out. I picked it up and looked at it closely. There were small bite marks in the roll. I examined the table. To my horror I found mouse droppings on the table, and when I took a closer look, in my purse as well.

Suddenly a light flashed in my head! It was me! I was responsible for bringing that mouse into our hotel room. I began to feel guilt. The mouse smelled the roll and had gotten into my bag when I put it on the floor in the restaurant. I never did keep that purse shut because it was such a bother.

Then I realized where the smell came from. The leather had absorbed the odor of the mouse droppings! I also knew that I could never get it clean enough to suit me.

I picked up the purse and dumped it into the garbage! What else could I do? Though I looked every where for another one like it, I never did find one.

THE END